Livina Press

A Literary Magazine

Issue Six: Natural World

Edited by Laci Felker

Masthead
Laci Felker | Founder | Editor-in-Chief

Paperback ISBN: 9798863810102

Contents

Poetry

Fiction

Creative Non-Fiction

Poetry

Grand Spectacle

Farrah Lucia Jamaluddin

Sunshine through mist cascades
in thin lines of yellow light-

The world's eye wakes, shifts,
amends its position
And you are invited to a grand spectacle:

I looked out to where sky meets sea,
and saw myself floating there in the
navel of the universe. My heart was
flesh and myth. My eyes mere portals
to multicoloured domains.
You were the entire world, another
Distraction from the most sublime
and I, for the first time, and the
ninety-ninth time, woke and knew
the Within would reach the Without.

The Cosmos sat back, contemplating
the night sky by a moonlit fire. Ze reasoned,
faithfully, that summer air was sweeter than
Winter's, and paired well with the image
of a woman in love. Yes,
one with dark and softened skin, free of a
rich man's determined sin. "She must be
Crafted darkness in a cup that warms
the belly before it burns the tongue
with a tinge of bitter relish."

Farrah Lucia Jamaluddin

A night sky in heat is for play,
for sultry dance by lanterned bay
A night sky in Winter is like
A lake filled with floating stars;
a crisp and misty hill up high,
a greying elder reading by candlelight.

The cosmos turned in pink
delight to watch the world
slip by. It stoked the flames
with a gloved and careful hand,
Tending to Nature's ways.

North

Kelsey Lister

The years have delivered me. North, on the cliff. To dream in a double bed. To dissolve into the sea. The Atlantic embraces my seventeen-year older body. Between each wave that melts— where have you been? Where did you go? Here. Shivering—steady and alive under the strawberry moon. Aligned with the constellations, I circle each star, connecting them on my back. My washed wishes melt on the shore. Small glimmers of this moment, bright between the grains. I've been returned. The tide pulls me with everything I couldn't see coming. Pushes me with all I've ever been.

Ritual

LeeAnn Olivier

"...how the innocent are bound to the damned" –Broken Bells

The dead wear moss wings, ringed
in whispers, the fabric of your skin
taut as a secondhand dress. Locusts
hum like madhouse lodgers speaking
in tongues, embers of fire and brim-

stone briars smoldering. You're a pilgrim
in the god's damned world where vapors pierce
the pines' lungs, the dark devouring
your dream-enclosed disguise in a duet
of hammers and drums. Over ravenous

caverns and wine caves, fat bright stars
graze like a gang of harbingers, an obstinacy
of bison hunched along the river, horns
and hooves haunting the badlands, bell,
book, and candle. Hell, hook, and idol,

his sepia lips plucking the pipes
of your spine like piano keys. He lassos
your bones like a shaman, a raptor
whose grammar feathers and plumes,
his birthmark barbed wire along his collar-

bone. Sometimes the innocent are bound
to the damned. All your bodies buckle,

your heart an unrung bell, the buck moon
white-knuckled, low and swollen like a tooth-
ache. The dead dream deeper still.

Brother Bear

Joseph M. Jablonski

Brother Bear, I seek
The curve of your claw,
A trophy, worthy to
Carve the deadwood soul from my chest.
For gnarled weeds of the world
Twist, bind my roots to the ground.
I seek my own kindling to make a spark!
Embers to burn, light for
The fire of my stars.

You charge,
Ursa Major flowing on your sooty fur.
You answer my call,
I with my metallic sword,
You with your five-fingered paw
Reading every thought,
Parrying every attack, and
I am struck with doubt, my swinging
Beginning to maul myself.
Your roar of the cosmos,
Without syllable, stirs me to tremble,
The ground moves,
Castles tumble,
And my own spirit
Awakens as I faint in hunted defeat.

For I see I was blinded
By past attempts,
We created palisades, marble balustrades

Slotted for the coward's arrow
While scrawling on the cave wall
In fearful ecstasy of flight.
My fathers - never could defeat you,
Ran away, hid
Behind stone and glass towers
Mirrors drowning out constellations,
Rusting our unused wonder, reduced to
Noise of nations,
Prisons of purposeless power.

Defeated in fear, I await
The killing blow of despair.
But your starry eyes see me
Truly: Alone, by myself,
Always burning like a supernova,
Silent in space's void, suspended
From steely words. The silence,
The haunting of the woods,
The loss of my language,
Pulls the planks from my eyes, and
For the first time I join
Nature in your invincible embrace.

It is here now I hibernate,
Rest in meditate, for
I now read your thoughts as you do mine,
Our once-combat now conversation
Joined by the leaves, the sky,
The wonder, the wood, the why,
Words blessedly lost, saved
Under the hooked blade
That sculpts with fierce and gentle way.

Untitled

Elijah Woodruff

we are all spirals; born out of nothing, we spin outward. into a
universe that is not great or cruel.
it is just a universe. a universe that is expanding and may one day
end and retreat back into the
smallest point of itself.

and after

perhaps the spiral will start again. Perhaps the atoms and the cosmic
dust and the planets and the
blood and the bone will fracture in the same place.

perhaps I will be your brother again

I hope this time you will let me play with you

that's all I wanted

want

An Evergreen Romance

Anushri Nanavati

I think winter wears gloves
When it picks off acacias
From the tips of tree fingers,
And scours birch skeins for
Whispered retinol as it swipes
The blue from a sky of colonial
Iris.

It' a strange combination, these
Plucked yellow suns and blue-eyed
Conquests, but winter is a harlequin
Who draws out cataracts
From a black top hat to bring forth
Snow.

I think winter grows stony when
Faced by evergreens sprawling out
With insouciance, like stubborn trawls
Of algae across a canvass of white
Blindness.

It's a strange idea, this romance
Of territories, this tug of pine needles
And bare-backed blizzards, but
Winter is a lover with swift sleighs
Of passion, and pinecones too
Might crave caresses.

groundskeepers

Ber Davis

take me back to those chilled summer nights,
where the sparks from our firepit glowed skyward—
snuffed out by the darkness as they reached for the stars.

take me back to those moth-eaten folding chairs,
where we sat back & smiled as the wind carried our howls to the
moon—
our cheeks reddened & chapped, our voices thick with jubilation.

take me back to those close-knit huddles,
where we stretched woolen blanket fibers across all our shoulders—
sharing stories of love, of sadness, of fear with our implicit promises
of secrecy.

take me back to those dusty old grounds,
where we tossed about a fragmented deer bone, chipped to the
marrow—
breathing in that oak-smoked air, breathing out that city-folk stress.

take me back to where time stood still because time was all we had.

When Summer Ends

Devon Neal

I wanted to tell you about August,
how the morning clings to the dark
and the trees swim in fog,
the silhouettes of their shoulders and limbs.

I wanted to tell you about how the sidewalks
where the gutters end grow wigs of rainwater,
how the lily, now de-bloomed,
strings spiderwebs between its green fingers.

I wanted to tell you how the heat comes still,
but the edges of dawn and dusk cool quicker,
and in the rain-haunted night, someone wrote
their damp name on the backdoor windows. ·

I wanted to tell you about August
and many other things like August,
waiting for us in our brief lives,
but not waiting for us at all.

Two Black Swans Basking in the Bay

Devon Webb

The sunrise
seen through your kitchen window
I glow, I glow
leaving kisses in the lion's mane
I wait, I wake,
I wax & wane.

Lost to a song
I long, I long
yearning for that gesture
so sweetly unfamiliar
aching to be your soft, your smile
your love when it doesn't come easy.

Sky painted in pastels, purple pink orange blue
I dream of you, I dream of you
will you come see my favourite view
will you walk my favourite route
is there a word for nostalgia in the moment
remembrance in the making
& can I share it all with you?

Two black swans
basking in the bay
backdrop of sunset streaming
they float & preen
I capture their beauty
as if they've found their way here just for me
& then around the corner on those

rocks with the perfect view
they swim back past across my panorama
three-sixty, all engulfing me
I'm adrift on ecstasy
those two black swans
alone in their ocean of glory
symbolising so unequivocally
the majesty of me & you.

Sea change

Jente H.

it's peaceful out here
on the ever changing tides
in the middle of the sea

i was following my heart
but instead i found a pearl
and a thousand kisses
waiting to return

and the hue of the lighthouse
is calling my name
but my body won't move
from the bottom of the ocean

To Make Another Me

N.A. Kimber

To what ends would you go
for that perfection you do seek
to craft in me?
What dark arts do you conjure
to conflate with sin
and strip the natural of its beauty
and put artifice on a pedestal?
Is the best the Earth has to offer
so inadequate to your eye?
Infectious perfection the splinter that has penetrated
and you do not dare deny.
What shall you carve and cleave
from my flesh and bones
to make another me?
What shall remain
when thorns are cut
and roots are torn?
When wilted petals are plucked
and wild leaves trimmed?
Will you be satisfied then?
Your ideal vessel
already on the verge of decay.
You've torn out the heart of her
with all the flaws
that got in your way.

girl goddess

Jasmine Young

my body's landscape is foreign to me.
not alien but mystical,
wrought with fruiting bodies of fungi,
footfalls of impish folk,
and scars leftover from the wintertime.

in the morning I pull back gauzy drapes
like dark gossamer,
hear the yawning of my people as they
wake. my downy
green hair is their first and last comfort.

in sleep our dreams are echoes of one
another. the moon,
she cools my sleep-warm body with
silvery rays. and then
I find the strength to bear fruit and flora.

I stare in amazement at the mountains of
me, careful to never
move. the sight of everything at once here
overwhelms, my
creations echoing some deific perfection.

In your safe hold

Maria Grace Nobile

In the folds of your arms, I release my soul.
Only wandering in your evergreen labyrinths, do I
Find my true self again.
Humbled by your sobering beauty and grandeur,
I remember my roots.
I am anchored deep in your soil.
My ancestors call out to me and give me rest.
I know this place because its history is embedded
In my membranes.
You are my refuge.
You are my hope.
I go back to nature to restore what is lost.
My soul.

Melancholia

SOUM

Vivaldi crescendos the passing of time
Winter, Spring, Summer and Fall dance beside
The turning of nature and life so entwined
How do we journey through seasons of life?

The passage of time in a flickering eye
Laid bare illusions of man's paradigm
Seasonal shifts of creation divine
Naïve to transitions of nature and mind

To mother's harmony we must incline
And seek the balance that nature designed
Too late does the folly of man realise
That winter has fallen upon all mankind

Egret Blossoms

Diane Webster

White egrets wander
across the dead tree's
island of roots
while each wades
into the pond …
searching.

The dead tree sags
as egrets nudge
memories of white
blossoms winging
wistfully to the ground.

the rockcliffe quarry

Jared Wong

from a rockcliffe quarry, summer solitudes spread in the heat.
amoebas sleep in the groundwork, fossilized in wine cellars, petrified
in mineral and unprocessed ore. in search of neighbourhood aval-
ons, children pour sand buckets of winter rain into the crater. offer-
ing. ritual. tithe. until the lowest strata is submerged. nature re-
encroaches.

waterways spring from the source, grow-up to become channels.
somewhere a tide awakens. sweeps footprints from the sand, erases
beaches. depositing lost flipflops and sunglasses amongst the reeds as
beacons. then rooftop lovers, midnight kisses, first date receipts,
rusty old pennies turn to foam. crest. heave. turn to rapids.

water-levels rising, berms of silt and hand painted pebbles form
secret coves. waiting for crescent moons and nautic gods to notice.

along a pristine surface, pomponettes drift across the epicentre.
never invoking wake. the quarry exhales. pauses. invites light to the
trenches. towards deep-water blooms. lone stars. aquatic heavens.
botanical worlds left to be observed by stargazers, outlaws, paddle-
boarders.

On a Snowy Evening

(An Ekphrastic Acrostic)

I stop to listen for the owls.
Have deer been here, these tracks?
Promises to owls come easy,
to fellow human travelers, not so much.
Keep crunching through the snow-cold night all silver-blue
and star-lit. Walk down
miles of hidden roads not taken, hard
to see in this white moonscape full of owl-song.
Go where depressions lead, frost-covered furrows.
Before I left tonight
I thought of you.
Sleep. By morning I'll be far away.

Snow Geese Rise

Tim Murphy

The content of dreams
from better days.
Walking beneath the sun
in a high desert oasis
one early spring morning.
The cold clings
to bones and the land.

Sage brush runs
for miles to the east.
A long-armed
fault block mountain
reaches beyond sight
to the west, frames
a vast azure lake.

I pan the water's edge
scan the middle.
A white floating mass
crawling slowly in place
until a glittering mirage
alights my vision
snow drifting upwards
to its origin sky.

As the geese rise I hear
many cries one echo
through the landscape.
They approach

Snow Geese Rise

where I stand
and witness
as they render
the sky white
and moving.

Dead End

Brandon Shane

Every morning, my mother would watch the snowfall,
all the windows were blackened but one, like a submarine
barely under the surface. Father had gone, and so had
the seasons, even in the winter it was no less summer.
She drank bourbon as fire would rage in the furnace,
a stomach full of wood, charring her intestines stone,
Light was meaningless, as were hallways and stairs,
the silence became a virus that swung us like tender
hulls rising to the cosmos as it climbed a rogue wave.
I sat beside her, amber eyes soldering in perpetuity,
hand on my forehead to check for a temperature,
and then the whip away as if her job had been done.
We scurried like coal orphans,
remembering the father with black lungs,
gazing at broken glass, shivering as the home chilled.
Alcohol soon carried down our throats,
moon after moon we became lunar eclipses,
but instead of the snow, we watched encumbered trees
sway as white frost hit the ground like bird eggs.
She was not cruel, but a treasured porcelain doll,
dethroned after an invasion of life's most toxic malady,
and all the grass grew, bushes became silos for possums,
father an author without texts, a prophet without memory,
all of us disciples who have forgotten the path
that led us to the avalanche.

IV. A Harsh Winter

Joseph Blythe

How the snow tumbles in a harsh winter,
Burying me alive.
I have felt its forgetful, icy clamour all my days,
My summer days, my winter days,
My autumns and my springs.
I have thought of the crystals that make each flake,
Dreamed of wearing one encrusted in a ring.
How the world became a bedsheet
Frozen 'round our fragile frames,
Feeling like a prison gate
Clanging shut in our face.
The snow falls, clumps of cloud,
Blinding my eyes, reflecting the sunlight,
Freezing me to death.

I sat beneath swathes of cloud,
Thick and foreboding and
Bursting like blossoms,
Snow falling pink as lips.
Clouds once fragile and exploding with light
Whipped and contorted by winds.
They dump and tumble,
Fall and fumble,
Quietly thunder.
The clouds above wear the faces of flowers,
The petals below are broken bodies.
And I think how beautiful the clouds were,
And how I wish they were here forever and ever.

Joseph Blythe

I was not sitting, waiting to be saved,
Or crucified.
Merely watching passers-by with a fire in my eye,
A blaze uncontrolled that set the world aflame,
Melting all the snow away –
How you relish the sunblaze!
I was sitting, waiting for a storm to pass.
I sheltered under branches.
A fire in the sky drove the snow and rain away
And we met, our two blazes, and we embraced,
Became one,
A fire in a flood.

Fiction

Birch Among the Asters

Holland Zwank

The girl from the leaves was the strangest person the town had ever seen. She didn't like to be referred to as a girl, wearing pants much more than she was supposed to, yet she still wore skirts. People asked for her name daily and she would say "Cedar" and they would tell her it wasn't a girl's name, to which she always responded with "well I am not a girl, but it is my name nonetheless" and people would scoff before leaving her alone once again.

Mrs. Aster told her sons every day not to go to her house. The grass was unruly instead of the strict cuts everyone else held. The house had become overcome with plants of a thousand colors, a rainbow stretching between the windows of flowers while every other house was in its row with the white plaster paint and black tilted roof.

True to her commands, Mrs. Aster's sons never went to her house. She would watch her oldest help the younger limp along, always sick. She was certain he was sicker now that the girl from the leaves had arrived, but no one believed her.

"Why," Mrs. Aster said one day while holding the Passages close to her chest and looking out her window as the hands of the girl from the leaves touched another vine that had stretched over their joined fence, but didn't pass into the Aster's backyard, "she is allowed to live there, I will never know."

"Yes, yes," the ladies agreed and nodded along with her, clutching their Passages to their chests while rattling off stories of people who had gone mad after talking to the girl from the leaves.

Every morning, Mrs. Aster went to get her mail and the girl from the leaves would be standing there, getting her own with a different flower crown winding its way across her head slowly, smiling.

"Good morning, Mrs. Aster," the girl from the leaves would say.

Mrs. Aster rarely replied.

"It's a lovely day, Mrs. Aster."

"It's going to rain," Mrs. Aster would say because often it was.

The girl from the leaves would smile and look up at the sky. "Yes, it is. If your sons want to come and help me with my garden after that would be nice."

"My sons will never be allowed in a spinster woman's house."

"I am not a spinster nor a woman, Mrs. Aster. My name is Cedar, and I am just a person," the girl from the trees would say, and Mrs. Aster would scowl instead of respond. "Have a good day, I'll see you in the morning."

After a few months, Mrs. Aster stepped outside to see the girl from the leaves standing in front of her with a purple, yellow, and white bouquet.

"This is for you and your sons, Mrs. Aster. They grew just this morning, and they were telling me how they yearned to be in your house. I hope you would take care of them. They very much would like to be loved by you."

Mrs. Aster took the bouquet and stuffed it down the trash can after the girl from the leaves left, her sons watching.

"You are not to talk to her."

And they both nodded as they always did while tightening their ties, Mr. Aster coming down the stairs with his Passages in hand. They would get in the car and take a trip to the Sermon where Mrs. Aster always asked the Passages to take the girl from the leaves away and she would come home with her husband and scowl as the girl from the leaves would be standing in her own front yard, wave, and keep talking to the trees that would stretch into the sky.

The next day, the girl from the leaves came back up to her house, in pants and with hair pulled back so tightly she almost looked like a man. Her chest looked flat that day, as she held another bouquet in her hands. It was filled with long flowers, the same color as the time before as the girl once again held it out for Mrs. Aster.

"These are for you, Mrs. Aster. They woke up this morning

begging for your love. Why, they are telling me right now that they would love to live in your house. Would you take care of them for me?"

Mrs. Aster snatched them from her hand, put them in an empty vase, and left them to dry, hoping that that would keep the girl from the leaves away.

"Why, she won't leave me alone!" Mrs. Aster told the other women as they flipped through their passages. "She stopped coming over with flowers, but she still talks to me every morning! If I weren't so strong with the Passages, I would tell her plants that they are lost with her. Why, they grow so big, I can hardly see the next house!"

"Yes, yes!" the other women agreed and nodded, sharing stories of the plants they had seen the girl from the leaves bring to other families, though none as much as Mrs. Aster.

"My husband can hardly believe his eyes, why he tried to get the newest ones to turn grey this morning by reading them the Passages. My oldest son told me he thought that we ought to take her to Sermon, so she hears the good words of the Passages herself and learns."

"Yes, yes!" the other women agreed.

"Why, but I won't invite her," one said, and the others nodded in agreement. "She's too odd, that one. I would betray the Passages, why someone else ought to do it, who she hasn't bothered yet."

"Yes, yes!" the other women agreed.

So, none of them invited her to the next sermon, where Mrs. Aster scolded her youngest son for coughing so much, covering his mouth with a napkin. He had gotten sicker even yet with the plants dying in the house, surely that was the girl from the leaves' plan. To poison them all with dying plants.

Mrs. Aster threw away the plants as soon as she got home.

"Why, Mrs. Aster," the girl from the leaves said, "the trees told me that they look at yours and feel so sad. Come, let your sons come pick some fruit and let it grow from my garden. They will flourish in only a day, and your sick son will surely get better if you let them grow. The trees keep telling me so."

"Your trees are the devil, girl," Mrs. Aster snapped, clutching her papers to her chest as she shut her mailbox. "Keep them away from mine, they are very happy, and my son does not need your medicine."

"Why, but just yesterday I heard him coughing while I was in the backyard. Won't you take a few flowers today, and let them live in your house?"

"A girl like you ought to follow the Passages and get married, young lady. Do not worry about my sons."

"Why, Mrs. Aster, you know I'm not a girl. I'm just a person. Look!" A yellow and purple flower sprung up over her arms, stretching out and Mrs. Aster took a step back, holding her papers tighter. "Won't you take them, Mrs. Aster? They tell me how good they are for the health of others. Surely, you must believe the words of plants over me. Why, your trees are very healthy, they've sang it every morning! Take these flowers?"

Mrs. Aster watched the flowers fall to the ground, leaving them there.

"She ought to leave town," Mr. Aster said, watching the girl from the leaves pick the flowers up sadly, the skirt she was wearing that day billowing in the breeze while she walked back to her house. "She's no good here."

Mrs. Aster nodded, hearing her youngest son cough once more from upstairs. She would take him to extra sermons, the girl from the leaves must have cursed him, he could hardly walk anymore or stand without fainting.

The Aster's took him to the Preacher who took one look at the youngest son and cast straight into the waters.

"You were right to stop taking her flowers, surely they are making her sick, let us keep him, we will heal him."

The women read their Passages with fervor, sometimes Mr. Aster and their eldest son would join too, all hoping that it would help the Sermons.

"My apologizes, Mrs. Aster," the girl from the leaves said in the morning, "about your son. Please, take some of these flowers! They are crying for your love. Look how they yearn for you, Mrs. Aster. Take them so they might survive!"

Mrs. Aster held her Passages between them. "Why, spinster, you have made my son sick! Your flowers have done nothing for him, my trees tell me that!"

"Please, Mrs. Aster, take them! They will not make it without you!"

She left the flowers behind, the girl from the leaves holding onto them tightly before heading back to her garden, waiting for the mail the next day.

"Mrs. Aster, I have loved being your neighbor, but I think it is time for me to live somewhere else. My flowers cannot stay here anymore. Might I ask that you take this white one, just this single flower?"

"Take it with you or let it wilt, girl, I will not make my son sick."

"Why, but Mrs. Aster, you *are*. Please, take the flower. I will not ask again."

"And I say take it with you!"

The girl from the trees nodded. "I understand. I will see you tomorrow for the last time, Mrs. Aster."

Her son came home in the morning, looking healthier than he had in years. Mrs. Aster ran to hug him, and he stepped away.

"Give me a hug! You have been sick!"

"If I hug you, I will get sick again," he answered, looking at the empty house which the trees had receded from as the girl from the leaves walked further down the street. "I must be going, or I will die if I stay, I'm sorry."

Mrs. Aster reached to grab him, holding her Passages out. "But the Sermons!"

He held his own book up. "I will read my Passages every night from the trees, just as you do, as if I am with you. My name is Birch, and I am just a person from the trees. Please accept my flower, or I must go."

Mrs. Aster only stared at the flower with purple, white, and yellow petals that he held out.

"You are my son!"

"I am a person. I must go now. I can't go inside, or I will surely get sick again. If you change your mind, I will bring you flowers back and see if I can live, but until that day, I must go with Cedar."

Mrs. Aster dove through her trash, willing the old flowers to grow back to prove that her son could live in the house, but she could hear the faint crying from them as her son continued to walk down the street, taking a flower from the girl from the leaves and watched it grow back in his own hands.

Lizard Wizards

H.E. Shippas

Abstract: Organisms of the class *Reptilia* are latent wielders of mana. Several experiments have come to light, connecting the idea that the common ancestor for mana users is not from the class *Mammalia* (Ogast, 1765) but still originates from the phylum *Chordata*. The compiled evidence gives credit to the hypothesis that reptiles can use mana naturally, versus human's manual use via external sources. While the exact source of mana use is still unknown, there are theories that might help us understand the origin of magic and how to better incorporate it into our biology.

Introduction

Since 1008, humans have been able to wield magic through the help of incantations and geometric drawings, with no other animals being known to wield as we can. Nothing in our biology determined what could possibly cause the use of magic, but it was theorized that our mana came from the Earth. As technology advanced, we were able to incorporate mana into our daily lives, which was able to reveal our theories were right: the mana we used for magic came from the Earth. All the magic we used went back into the Earth, similar to the water cycle. There is no way for us to naturally store the mana, so our magic is limited (Stotrix et al., 1798).

Current experimentation has shown evidence that, while we cannot store mana naturally, there are other organisms that can and use mana in benign ways for living (ex, color changing, slight body morphing, poison creation). Evidence has led to the theory that these animals do not use higher levels of magic due to the low level of brain activity and sapience of the subject (Arick and Crusim, 1998). While evidence of magic use outside of reptiles does exist, reptiles currently have the strongest amount of evidence towards being added for the "List of Magical Organisms."

Experiments

First experiment came from the University of South Hadia in what was labeled "unrelated evidence" of the original experiment. Dr. Marcuson Ubarin was experimenting with cancer cells on *Pantherophis guttatus*, or corn snakes. After a terrorist attack left South Hadia frozen for two weeks, the subjects were found to be unharmed from the magical attack and thriving, internal of the cages was 86 degrees fahrenheit and full of mice bones. After footage was recovered, it was found that the snakes were never affected by the magical blast and continuously teleported frozen mice from the outlying labs to their cages in intervals of 2-3 days. While Ubarin was unable to be thawed out, the research was repeated by his second in command (Dr. Laris Egumanor) under a controlled environment 3 times to find the snakes to have protected themselves from magical freezing, but natural freezing caused natural defenses rather than magical ones. No mana use was detected when temperatures decreased gradually, but mana-pulse infliction of freezing caused a counter-spell reaction in the corn snakes. Continuous magical freezing led to the corn snakes to create a new habitat that allowed them to get food without having to leave their environment, which would explain the teleportation (Egumanor and Ubarin, 2023).

Second experiment came in parts from the Institute of Desert Magic in Uwopora with the *Crocodylus arenus*, or sand crocodile. Original experimentation implied that the sand crocodile traveled through glass tunnels in the sand that were made with the friction from the high speed of their movement (Prixeor, 1867). Through mana detection, it was found that the sand crocodile was using rudimentary heat exchange spells to increase their skin temperature to 3100 plus degrees fahrenheit, silica melting temperatutes(Unesim et al., 2019). This allows the crocodile to move faster, as well as burn any prey it may come into contact with. It is currently unknown why the species only uses the spells in the sand, rather than utilizing the magic when above ground. Recreating the environment the crocodile uses for travel has been inconclusive; the crocodile does not travel when in captivity, only traveling on top of sand when around humans (Donesin and Unesim, 2021). Trackers placed on crocodiles in the desert have been shown to have upticks in mana consumption at intervals of fast traveling underground (Vero, 2020).

The final experiment came from Domity's School of Magical Research. A paper titled "Microdimensional Pockets in the Stomachs of Modern Ophidians" was published by Sir Erish of the reptilian department, first citing the "ouroboros effect." This is a rare phenomenon found in less than 5% of all modern day snakes. 95% of the time, when a snake starts to eat itself, it will die. In a study of 1156 snakes with mana trackers on their tails, 58 of those trackers vanished once the snake was half-consumed. Attaching a micro-infrared camera showed a void inside of these snakes; no heat or cold was detected in this subspace. It is currently unknown as to what the function of this space would be, or why it would only be active during such a traumatic event (Erish, 2016).

Conclusion

As more grants are submitted for magical studies with reptiles, it is important to remember why these studies help the magical community. If we can understand how creatures with smaller brains can innate use magic, we could find a way for us to use magic without spell components or drawing runes or incantation. An innate use of magic could allow us to save on resources needed to cast higher-cost mana spells.

Papers that were archived due to inclusion of "dragons" should be reconsidered for credibility. Our present technology gives credence to the idea that there might have been giant lizards that used mana to take flight or defend themselves using fireball spells. As technology advances and our use of mana becomes more complicated every day, we should take a step back and look at what nature intended for our use of mana to be.

. . .

Principal Investigator Comments

Review paper approved. Studies will open up towards paleon-tology as well. If animals in the reptilian group can use magic, there is a chance dinosaurs were able to cast spells as well. This begs the question: what spell was so strong that could wipe out a bunch of magical dinosaurs?

The old man who walked out of the foam and the seaweed

Ben Coppin

Where did I come from? Good question. I didn't always exist, you know. Before I existed I used to write stories. I wrote about all kinds of things, but never anything terribly interesting. Never anything anyone else would want to read. I wrote one story about a sunflower. I liked that one, but I didn't think anyone else would.

Shh. Don't ask questions. It's impertinent to interrupt your elders. I know it doesn't make sense: but then what does?

So anyway, there I was sitting in my shack by the sea when I had an idea for a story. It would be about an old man, a man with a long white beard and no hair on the top of his head. Yes, like me. Just like me, actually.

He'd be happy, most of the time, and sometimes sad, and he'd worry maybe more than he should, but he'd do his best to be kind and friendly, and that was what would make him interesting.

Oh, you don't think those things sound interesting enough? Well, what would you know? You're still very young.

Anyway, perhaps the most interesting thing about him would be his grandchildren. He'd have, ah, let's see, how many would he have? Oh, two? Yes, that sounds right. I think I wrote him that way. He had two grandchildren. Perhaps a couple of children as well — I can't remember.

And those grandchildren? They'd be amazing. They'd be the future of his world. And the present of his world, for a while. He wouldn't live forever, you know. He'd try to, but he wouldn't. No-one does, as a general rule.

So he wrote me, this man in his shed by the sea. Shack? Is that what I said? Shed, shack. Same thing. This man in his hovel by the sea, he wrote me into his story, and that's how I came to be. I just, kind of, emerged from the foam and the seaweed. No, not naked, I was wearing jeans and a t-shirt, and I knew what I needed to do right away, as soon as I walked on to the beach: I needed to come here, to this town you children live in, and meet you both. So I caught a train. They had trains that went all the way to the sea in those times. And you didn't need to pay to ride on them. The writer didn't write me any money. He could have done, but he didn't. So I had to get a job and work, but it didn't stop me getting to you, because, like I said, the trains were free.

So there you are, my little ones. That's the story of how I came to be, and more importantly it's the story of how I came to be your Grandpa.

Your parents? Oh, I don't know their story. You'll have to ask them. But you can bet it'll be a good one.

The Door by the Ocean

Jeff Presto

It was never supposed to be anything more than a joke.

Justine sat out on the balcony of her parent's fourth-story hotel room and stared out at the ocean. She watched as the waves crashed down in the distance and took notice of the water as it pushed its way further up the shore. Several news helicopters circled over the hotel and jockeyed for position to film the beach and the boardwalk below. Luckily for pilots, their target was not one that could be easily missed.

The thick green wall of seaweed that had washed ashore could be seen from miles away. Even from the hotel balcony, its presence was unmistakable. The algae mass towered over the sandy banks and had anchored itself to dry ground through a network of small green tendrils. Marine biologists were already referring to the event as an anomaly, mostly due to the fact the seaweed was growing over itself in a distinct coiled pattern rather than drifting to shore in smaller clumps, and it soon became the topic of conversation for many of the tourists in the area. The seaweed snaked its way along the beach in the form of one long column before diverging off into several large strands. This was the reason for the helicopters. From the overhead view of the beach that was being shown by the local news, the seaweed resembled a giant hand stretching out from the water. Each day, the hand had crept a little closer towards the boardwalk and several of nearby hotels.

Justine's eyes remained on the coast. They widened with disbelief until she became startled by the sound of the patio door opening behind her. Her father walked outside to join her, half-empty bottle of beer pressed to his lips, as he gazed out towards the ocean. He was just as confused as anyone else, but he was also clearly fascinated by the event.

"I've never seen anything like it," he marveled.

"I don't think anyone has," Justine agreed. "How big do you think it's going to get?"

"No clue," he smiled, looking back over to Justine. "But that thing's big enough that you could drive a car down it."

There was probably close to forty feet of sand that separated the water's edge from the boardwalk, but the tangled green mess had bridged that gap in only a matter of days. In that time span, the growth had expanded to a width of nearly ten feet and was practically as tall as the wooden lifeguard stands that were set up along the coast. The growth showed no signs of stopping. Silently, Justine wondered to herself if that was even still a possibility.

Another helicopter roared as it flew by the hotel.

"Are you joining us for dinner tonight?" her father asked, finishing his beer. "Your mom and I are going to the buffet across the street if you want to come. Leaving in thirty."

"I'm not really that hungry," Justine lied. "I'll probably go and find something to eat later on tonight."

Justine had grown increasingly independent over the years and she was about to begin her freshmen year of college. Her parents did their best to respect this fact, within reason, but something as simple as eating separately was never an issue. Her father nodded at the response as if he had already known what her answer would be.

"Suit yourself," he replied, opening the patio door. "If that seaweed doesn't settle down, we might all be eating salads anyway."

Justine laughed as she followed her father back inside, but she found nothing about what was happening on the beach to be amusing. In fact, it terrified her. She continued to smile until she reached her bedroom and closed the door behind her. Only now was she able to let her guard down and drop the charade. The smile melted from her face as she laid down on her bed and stared up at the ceiling. There was no use in pretending that everything was okay.

It had been three days since Justine went down to the shore and drew a Ouija board into the sand. She had gotten the idea to do so when she had passed an old fortune telling booth on the western end of the boardwalk. The booth was closed when she walked by, but she found something both alluring and amusing about someone who claimed to be able to see into the future. Her life was already moving fast enough with college approaching, and she doubted very much that the words of a generous stranger would do anything to help. Still, it was a comforting thought. When she had finally arrived at the beach, the elaborate artwork was still fresh in her mind. She couldn't help herself as she traced her finger along the ground in the shape of a large rectangle.

Justine remembered glancing around the beach nervously, almost embarrassed by what she had planned to do, but felt relieved by the lack of beachgoers surrounding her. It was still too early for many of them to venture outside, her parents included, but she got to enjoy the sunrise in peace.

She was also able to work without any distractions.

The drawstring bag that she carried with her had been packed for the occasion. It contained several handfuls of broken twigs that were used to craft the letters of her board and a tennis ball to be used as a planchette. The features took a few minutes to construct. After glancing around the beach once more, Justine closed her eyes and placed her hand over the tennis ball.

If her parents had seen her doing any of this, she would have died from humiliation. It was an admittedly dumb thing to do, but for more reasons than she initially realized. She asked all the typical questions to the board, wondering if anyone was listening to her and asking whether she would enjoy her new school, but nothing happened. The tennis ball never rolled in any direction, and Justine gave up on waiting for it to do so. She stood up from the board and gazed out across the water as the rising tide rolled in and kissed her ankles. It wasn't until she looked down that she realized her board had begun to wash away. Justine had thought nothing of it, especially because the board didn't work, but this idea was quickly proven wrong in the days ahead. There was now a giant green hand that reached out of the ocean which covered the exact location of where her board had been. She had summoned this.

It was only now that she realized that she never closed the gate that the Ouija had opened.

Justine sat up in bed and cursed herself for being so careless. In this moment, she wished that she could be like the countless other girls her age who drowned out their anxiety and loneliness with a bottle of vodka or with a group of close friends. Even an uneventful day at the pool would be better than this. There were hundreds of other outlets that she could have channeled her frustrations into, but instead, she had chosen the one that involved the dead. Or Satan. Or whoever's arm was crawling up along the coast. She didn't even know or believe in anything that she was doing when she drew up the board; she just wanted to be heard. Now, she felt as if wanted to disappear.

Justine hurried to the corner of her bedroom and picked up her gym bag from the dresser. There was no time to waste. Her mind raced as she packed her bag with anything that she thought might be useful to battle the monstrous appendage along the coast. After a few minutes, her arsenal consisted of only a flashlight and a lighter. She struggled with her selection, but ultimately came to the realization that things needed to be settled the same way that they began. Nothing inside of the hotel could help her now. She knew that she had to fix this on her own.

Outside of her room, Justine heard her parents getting ready to leave for dinner and they shouted their goodbyes to each other from opposite sides of her closed bedroom door. Once she was certain that they were gone, Justine grabbed her things and quickly exited her room.

Reaching the boardwalk was the only thing left on her mind.

The helicopters had stopped roaming the skies as Justine neared closer to the coast. She jogged down South Main Street and could see the ocean ahead. A giant hill of brown and green seaweed loomed in the distance and a distinct salty rotten odor grew stronger as she approached. The seaweed had tangled itself around one of the fishing piers that jutted out from the boardwalk and now threatened to consume the central walkway as well. The bright yellow caution tape that roped off the area fluttered in the evening breeze.

Justine ignored the flimsy barrier and ran across the boardwalk until she reached the sand. There was no one outside patrolling the beach, but several vacationers watched from their hotel windows as she ran along the coast. Just a few feet away from the giant hand, Justine threw down her gym bag and began to draw.

The waves in front of her grew louder as she began to build her letters. She formed them out of whatever she found nearby. Clumps of seaweed, twigs, and sea shells were laid hastily in front of her as she dug around in her gym bag to find her tennis ball. The rising tide inched closer to the board each time she looked up, and if she didn't hurry, the board would once again be washed away. Her eyes widened as she retrieved the ball and placed it down on the board, but as Justine began to concentrate, she was quickly distracted by the sound of something shrieking nearby.

She glanced up and the giant hand seemed to be hissing at her.

Justine stared at the hand in disbelief as the mass of seaweed began to writhe. It sounded as if dozens of snakes were suddenly threatening her all at once, but beneath the hissing was the sound of something much worse. A voice whispered out to her from somewhere within the seaweed. It was soft and spoke slowly to her, but Justine felt her heart leap into her throat when the voice addressed her by name.

"Don't do this, Justine," the thing warned. "This is your moment. Don't throw it away."

Justine didn't answer. Had it not been for the heavy waves breaking in the distance, she would not have been able to look away. A series of low, flat thuds continued to slap the coast. The crashing waves directed her attention back to the ocean, and the tide had consumed nearly all the sand between the water's edge and the Ouija board. In a minute, it would all be gone.

"Leave," the thing whispered urgently.

The tennis ball began to wiggle in place beneath Justine's hand. She gripped it firmly and closed her eyes as she focused all her energy onto the Ouija board. She could sense something looming in front of her, but forced herself not to look.

"Close the gate!" Justine yelled as loud as could.

There was no time for her to repeat herself. As soon as she shouted the command, a large wave crashed down on top of her and sent her tumbling backwards. Justine's legs flew up over her head as she desperately fought to catch her breath. She spit out a large mouthful of salt water as she regained her balance and started to run. The Ouija board and her bag had both washed away, and dozens of shrieks were erupting from within the hand. The ground shook beneath her and Justine became fearful that she might lose her footing. One wrong move could send her tumbling to the ground for the seaweed to snare her. The thought being dragged underwater with multiple demonic entities shrieking in her ear sent her sprinting up the shore. By the time that she had reached board-walk and continued onto South Main Street, the sounds of splin-tering wood and a deathly hiss thundered loudly behind her.

When Justine turned back around, the beach was unrecogniz-able from only moments ago. The hand had completely retracted itself back into the ocean. Several deep claw marks were dug into the terrain from its heavy green fingers, leaving a series of shallow lagoons behind. The act seemed to defy logic and left Justine in a surreal and dreamlike state. As she continued to scan the coast, she realized that the fishing pier had been torn apart from where the several ropelike strands had attached themselves. Pieces of drift-wood bobbed about in the cold gray tides, and Justine considered herself lucky not to have ended up among the wreck of scattered debris.

The streets quickly flooded with cars and people, but Justine continued to stare out into the water. Even as the police arrived to gather statements from several people claiming to have witnessed the event, Justine's attention remained on the shore. Everything else could wait. Justine knew she wouldn't be able to sleep until she was certain the hand was gone for good. It was all too easy for her to imagine her hotel being crushed beneath the weight of a giant green palm.

When the tide started to recede, Justine had decided that she was finally comfortable enough talk to the police. There was no trace of the Ouija board or any of her belongings on the beach. All she could provide them with was a wild story that wouldn't be taken seriously, but it was the truth.

The portal had been sealed.

The helicopters had returned to the skies and circled the beach once more. Their search lights revealed nothing but sand, driftwood, and empty waters.

An Earth Elemental's Gift

Angela Patera

Clara was sitting on a bench at the town's playground, watching over her little sister, when a girl in a purple dress approached her.

Her blonde hair was tied up with ribbons—which matched the dress' color—in two braided pigtails. Her big gray eyes glistened and glimmered, full of wonder. She looked to be five, maybe six years old.

"Your necklace is very beautiful," the girl said in awe. "Did someone gift it to you?"

"Thank you," Clara said, smiling. "Yes, it was a gift. Someone special gave it to me. What's your name, dear?"

"Vanessa," the little girl said and sat down next to Clara on the bench. "What is your name?"

"My name is Clara."

"Who is this special person that gave it to you?"

Clara pursed her lips. Should she tell her? It's no secret that little children are curious creatures, asking about something and forgetting what had grabbed their interest a moment before, by shifting their attention to something else.

Clara hesitated sharing the secret which, so far, she has revealed only to her sister. And this girl was a complete stranger. Would it harm though? Vanessa would assume that Clara was inventing a tale on the spot, and possibly forget about it as soon as she went back to play whatever game she was playing before the necklace had caught her attention.

"You won't believe me, but an earth elemental gifted it to me."

"A what?" Vanessa asked confused.

"You could say it's something like a fairy of the earth, a forest spirit," Clara explained.

"A fairy? Whoa!" the little girl exclaimed with big eyes. "Does the necklace have magical powers?"

"No, I'm afraid not." A disappointed look painted Vanessa's face for a few seconds. Clara chuckled. "This happened many years ago. I was five, so your age."

"I'm six!" Vanessa corrected her.

"All right, I was one year younger than you," Clara conceded and gave her a small smile. She threw a brief glance at Emily, her sister, to check if everything was fine. All good, she was chatting with a girl beside the slide.

"How old are you now?"

"I turned sixteen a few months ago."

"Ohh, so you met the fairy eleven years ago."

"Correct. Anyway, I was a little girl and my parents and I had gone on a roadtrip. After a few hours of driving, our car broke down. My dad called a mechanic. He said he could be there in two hours at the earliest; first he had to finish some other repair. In addition, we were far out in the countryside, so it would've taken a while to arrive.

"I of course was bored. I asked my parents if I could go explore the area. They let me, but warned me not to go too far away. I walked for a quarter of an hour—I lost sight of my parents and the car in the first five minutes—and came across an opening, lurking at the edge of the road, with a path leading directly into the forest. My curious self couldn't resist. I walked on the path. The deeper I went into the forest, the more an odd feeling nagged in the back of my mind that someone was watching me."

"It was the fairy, right?" Vanessa cut in.

"Yes, as it would turn out. She was watching me, hiding where I couldn't see her. I quickly pushed aside that feeling though, to focus my full attention on the beauty of the forest. The sun shone through the canopy, bathing the green of the trees and forest ground in rich light, animating it. The flowers in all their magnificent colors and honey-sweet aromas, swayed with a dreamy elegance in the gentle breeze. Birds sang stunning melodies, seeds of dandelions sailed in the air with their ghostly parachutes. I know it sounds cliché, but the scenery had something magical about it."

"What does cliché mean?"

"Something that has often been said and is therefore not original anymore," Clara explained. She continued her story: "At some point, as I was striding toward a big white flower, I spotted a beetle on the ground. It was lying on its back, struggling to get to its feet. I helped it, gently turning it over. That's when the earth elemental appeared in front of me."

"What did she look like?" the little girl asked in a curious voice.

"I was just about to say," Clara said with an amused smile. "She had brown skin and green, moss-covered hair. She was dressed in a floor-length dress made out of leaves. It had intricate design. Some parts of the dress were decorated with green gemstones and she wore a headpiece adorned with those same glistening jewels. A pink flower was tucked behind her ear. Her ears looked just like elvish ones, long and pointy. Her nose was small and narrow, her lips thin but delicate. Her eyes were green and glimmered like stars. They radiated kindness and behind them lurked a powerful, ancient intelligence. She had a most serene expression on her face," she paused, lost in memories. "I wasn't afraid of her. On the contrary, her presence calmed me, it felt like I was in a trance."

"It sounds like she was very beautiful," Vanessa said.

"Yes, indeed she was," Clara agreed. "She was the first to speak: 'Hello little one, you who helped a forest's creature in need. What is your name, kind human?' she said in a tranquil voice that matched her appearance.

" 'My name is Clara. Who are you?' I replied.

" 'I am Lifalun,' she said, to which I asked:

" 'Are you a fairy?'

" 'I am an earth elemental. I am the guardian of this forest,' she said and put her hand, palm forward, on my forehead and closed her eyes. It felt like butterflies were fluttering in my skull while she did that. After a moment she lowered her hand and held it in the air, palm upward. To my surprise a necklace appeared out of nowhere—"

"The one you're wearing!" Vanessa exclaimed cheerfully.

"Correct! She hung it round my neck and said: 'You are a good-hearted soul, Clara. Not many humans are. I gift you this necklace, the pendant of which is a jade gemstone. It shall remind you of your uniqueness and it is a promise that you are at all times welcome in my forest,' she said and gave me a warm smile. I smiled back. A few seconds later she vanished right before my eyes."

"Whoa!" Vanessa said and was deep in thought for a moment. "Do you think she would gift me a necklace too, if I ever saw her?"

"If you are a good person and kind to mother nature, to her animals and plants, then yes; I think you would get Lifalun's respect and therefore you'd be honored with her gift.

"Oh, yeah, that makes sense," Vanessa said, chuckling. "I will try my best, nature deserves to be treated well by us humans."

Clara smiled at her and shifted her gaze to her sister, who was running toward them in that moment.

"Hey Emily. Have you had enough of playing? Do you want to go home?" Clara asked her.

"No, I want to play a little more!" she said and looked at Vanessa. "Hello, who are you?"

"Hello Emily, I'm Vanessa. Would you like to play with me?"

"Yes, I'd love to!"

"Awesome!" Vanessa replied and both girls sprinted back to the playground.

Clara watched them run away, a fond smile lighting up her face.

Playing Pretend

Ashley Mina

When Lena lays down in the dirt, she feels like someone else.

She'd placed herself under the apple tree just at the edge of her backyard. Still in her school clothes, the reddish-brown soil stained the underside of her hand-me-downs as leaves crumpled in her hair and native grass tickled at her nose. She wanted to know if the brown squirrel she'd seen that morning climbing inside the branches was still there.

After ten minutes of laying in silence waiting for a tail twitch or the sharp chitter of teeth, Lena grew bored. Mind wandering, she closed her eyes and fell into the feeling of being a stranger within her own body.

Here, she is Lena the witch. With all manner of potions and trinkets tucked away in her rucksack. She knows that when she grows thirsty from resting, her large glass vial of water will replenish her. She knows that any hunger that may befall her will also be provided for, if she dared knock a ripe apple down from the tree sheltering her head from the chilly breeze. She doesn't yet know the spell her mother uses to transmute those ingredients into apple pie though. Which is a shame.

Lena reaches into the bag, feeling more than seeing the large tome within. Its binding is as old and frail as a crone's greying hair, half falling apart in her small hands. She pulls it out of the darkness where it belonged and onto her chest. It was a cursed thing with all manner of horrors within. The great scholars of this witchcraft scoffed at the mere sight of her agony when she cringed away from it's magics; telling Lena that it was important for every young apprentice to learn the old ways of long division. Such sigils burned her eyes when she gazed upon them.

$42 \div 2 =$

$90 \div 30 =$

$50,000 \div 0 =$

Mind dividing into mirrored fractures of sanity, Lena shook her head hoping the numbers would spill out of it. What did it mean. What does any of it mean. She huffed and her breath caught in the air. Goosebumps appeared on her arms. Lena the witch closed her eyes again because pretending to be her meant that she would feel compelled to do her homework and that was worse then being the real Lena.

So here is Lena the forest fairy. Gentle fingers sway in time with the blades of grass so that they never quite get to touch her. The breeze catches on her translucent wings and she becomes weightless in an instant. Floating away and into the branches of the apple tree until she spy's Archibald the brown squirrel, her steed, curled into a protective ball and happily asleep. Lena felt bad about waking him, but she needed him. As princess of Apple Forest, Lena could never be caught flying like all the other fairies. She was better than them, mostly because she had previously been able to survive reality shifting math magics, and they had never heard of them. Lucky people. But also, she was scared of heights and it felt better to cling to the furry back of a trusted companion than risk her own wings failing her. That's why she was on the ground in the first place, but if any fairy asked, it was because she was hunting scary beetles in the grass.

Just as Lena the forest fairy climbed upon a half-asleep Archibald, a horn rang out clear and sharp. The scary beetles were attacking and she was needed in the fight! The two, always prepared for sudden war, leaped into action. Scaling the bark of the tree and pushing through the roaring crowd of other fairies, Lena saw it. Ichor-backed and heaving with apple tree killing sicknesses, it locked its eyes on hers and charged. While other fairies took to higher branches, Lena and Archibald meant to rear up to show off the strong swipe of his claws, but when her steed went vertical and the princesses' stomach lifted into her throat, she slipped off. Wings sticky with scary beetle venom, Lena had realised too late that they were surrounded and now she was

Falling,
  Falling,
    Falling.
Until she hit the rock bottom of her hubris and become yet another stranger still.

Laying at the base of the apple tree, she is Lena the guardian of this forest. The looming tree washes its shadows overtop of her, eclipsing the waning sun in dazzling patterns of leaves and branches and swaying apples. She lays, arms crossed to touch her shoulders like she'd seen movie monsters in coffins do. But Lena was no monster, simply she was eternal. Body succumbed to damp ground. Mushrooms and moss growing over her skin. She had just awoken from hibernation and right now she was too weak to lift a finger, yet too strong to lose her mind to the equations plaguing her. They were like thorns pricking at the edges of her brain. Retched math, what use does she have for such a horrid thing when she is but the guardian of this small patch of wildness.

Wisdom courses through the autumn wind and into Lena the guardian's thoughts. The sky darkens as it tells her that the wilderness is like math. Infinite and overwhelming. Hungry to have its mysteries be solved. Lena's stomach rumbles at the thought of hunger and in the distance, thunder echoes it. Far off from shelter and fearing for lightning, Lena tries to wiggle away when the spattering of gentle rain begins to soften the moss holding her in place. She's almost free when she hears the resounding crack of a branch snapping in two.

A cloaked figure steps up beside Lena wielding a familiar frog patterned umbrella as a shield against the rain. For as suddenly as Lena wanted to be rid of her duties to the forest, she now holds those responsibilities dear. She watches, already pouting, as her mother kneels beside her in the leaves, hands steepled in prayer.

"Oh, precious daughter, please deign to join me for setting the supper table."

"But mom!" Lena complains, "I'm busy being the guardian of the forest."

"I know, Leeny-baby, but dinner's in ten minutes. Up and at 'em, come on."

Lena the guardian thinks it over for a moment. Going inside after a long day of laborious pretending might not be so bad. At least in there she can play a villainous scullery maid who steals fingerfuls of mashed potatoes.

Appearing in an instant at the questioning gaze of her mother, she becomes Lena the girl again. Where she was once quiet and unassuming in the underbrush of the apple tree, she is now real and hungry and shivering as her clothes become soaked. Her mother offers her a hand and with her assistance, Lena sits up and slings her backpack over her arms.

When they're both standing, it only takes a glance between the two of them before they are sprinting as fast as they can back to the house. Kicking up the freshly appeared mud onto the space where Lena's body once sheltered it.

Lore of the Forest

Jessica Ungeheuer and Alethea Lyons

Time of day is lost on me. The woods remain dark. Muted. My lungs burn with the cool air that labours through them. My fingers are numb, as I struggle to keep the tension on the bow. My head, dizzy from the blood loss. My left leg, weak. Only reminded of my injury by the stabbing agony that rains through my nerves like a thousand knives as I apply more weight, steadying my aim.

I know it is there…I have had the same strange sensation since entering the woods. Something within the thick brush, prowling… waiting. It is the creature. A demon. The monster that poisoned our sacred woods.

Closing my eyes, I search for my centre. The essence of the woods. I need to hear it. A technique taught to me by my father, and his father before him. The pounding pulse of my heart that radiated in my ears subsides, replaced by the small rustle of leaves as the wind passes through the thick canopy above, the running of water from the nearby stream, the fluttering of small wings in the distance, a soft beat in the sod. Note all of them. Find the sound out of place… There!

I open my eyes, barely escaping the demon's maw. Pain surges through my leg. I let out my held breath, clenching my teeth. I let the discomfort distract me. I didn't see it. A claw.

Searing pain stabbed into my ribs. The ground beneath me, gone. My movement only stopped by abrupt pain in every muscle of my back as it slammed into the hard surface of the tree that caught me. I reach for my knife, nestled still in the waist of my belt. My mind wanders to my village…

.   .   .

It is a small village, nestled in the countryside, only a day's ride away from the capital. We are blessed, not just by the close proximity to the capital, but by the forest just behind our gates. It provides all the resources we need. Wood to build our homes and heat our hearths. Fresh water from the stream that runs through the village centre. And plenty of game for meat to feed our bellies and furs to clothe our bodies.

The forest also provides a very special plant. The *salus vita*. A small herb that only grows in these woods. It has multiple medicinal properties, making it popular for use by the apothecaries of the capital in a wide variety of potions and ointments.

As the population in the village and the capital grew over the years, the need for our special plant did too. Soon strangers, sent by apothecaries trying to cut out the village from the profits, began to send people to acquire it. That's when the troubles started.

At first it was small stories of strange encounters. The trees were moving in the forest, blocking their ability to find the herb. So in response, people began burning the woods. Then the attacks happened. Each time it was a different animal. A bear. A wolf. An enraged stag. People were dying, and in turn so was our village. Unable to have access to the source of our fortune and life, the village lost its main value for trade and supplies. So many people have become reliant on our little plant, that if we cannot resolve this issue, too many will suffer the consequences.

It was then that the village chieftain came to my door. Pleading that I go into the woods and kill the demon infecting the once pure forest. I had not hunted in many years, giving in to age. However, I was the last of the *old ways*. Last of the ones that understood our balance with the forest. I begrudgingly grabbed my bow and hunting knife, heading into the woods.

* * *

The lore of the forest is simple. Live and die and live again.

I am the forest and it is me. My touch brings birth and death, encouraging plants in spring and withering them in winter. Hunter

59

and prey both shelter under my canopy. I have been here for centuries, existing.

I alight upon a maple tree, its leaves just on the turn to sunset colours. My talons grip its bark as I open my beak and raise a coarse caw. I can feel the life pulsing within the maple, even as it readies for sleep. There is a thread of darkness there too, a rot eating away at its heart. It is the humans' doing.

Whatever is in the forest becomes me and whatever is in me becomes the forest. Humans brought this disease and it spreads faster with every passing season. Before they came, I had no concept of anger, of revenge, of hate. They taught me these bitter lessons. Unless I am rid of them forever, their greed will destroy us.

When they first came, I welcomed them as I would any creature travelling south for the winter. I sheltered them from storms and fed them from my bounty. They respected my lore and learnt to live as one with me.

But as generations passed, our connection frayed and I suffered for the trust I showed them. They tore leaves from branches and ripped roots from the ground. They gutted my children and left their bodies to rot. Then they came for my trees, the bones of my being. They hacked them apart with snaggle-toothed metal and turned them to ash with fire and rage.

Humans were easy to catch then. I took the guise of the hunters living within my boundaries - wolf, lynx, bear, and eagle. Easily disorientated, humans became ensnared by my dark labyrinth. Their corpses fertilised fir and pine. Wildcats and canines gnawed their bones, licking out the marrow.

Yet soon their rich meat turned sour in our bellies. For each I killed, they murdered a dozen of mine, a never-ending stream of fire and iron. Where once humans dwelt peacefully in my shadow, now they sent their youth to haunt and steal from me. They learnt to be silent, smearing dirt across their faces and covering themselves with my leaves. Yet I can always smell them, their putrid sweat filling the air with the stench of fear. 'Demon' they call me and 'Demon' I shall be until my forest is safe again.

There is one near now. He is clever, moving through the trees as though he belongs, smelling of honest labour. But he is human and for me to live, he must die.

My limbs tense, ready to hunt. Hollow, like a dead tree felled by lighting, I burn and spark. I will rip and tear with tooth and claw. I will drag chunks of flesh to the edge of my domain, where the trees meet the plains, and leave them there to decay as a warning. To consume them is a respect they do not deserve. I want no more of the humans tainting me or my folk.

I move closer, staying small in the guise of a squirrel. The trees mask my approach, rustling their leaves as I leap from branch to branch. They close ranks behind me, cutting off my prey's escape. The air grows dim as they knit their branches together forbidding the sunlight entry. I summon the luminescent mists of the other-world. A thousand eyes watch, pinpricks glimmering from gashes in trunks and burrows in the dirt. Silent still, I can sense their thoughts. I am their champion. Their salvation.

The human is knelt in a clearing, an iron tool in his hand. I shudder as he plunges it into the earth. It burns, as though he stabbed it into my heart. His breath hangs in the air before him and he tugs stolen furs tighter around his torso. Deceptive eyes, mimicking the sky's blue, dart back and forth.

I drop to the ground, legs stretching, bones popping into place as claws burst from my paws. My fur changes from deep brown to mottled beige. My bushy tail stretches, the fur thinning. Whiskers twitch. My tongue lolls over the sharp teeth of a predator. The change is as natural to me as breathing, the form of a lynx my favourite in which to hunt.

Like a cat with a mouse, I want to play with him. Terrify him. I shall let this one live and return to his den. Warn others. They must learn the lore of the forest. Live and die.

The trees sense my intent and move aside, creating a tunnel for him to flee down. Their branches curve overhead, twisting and melding. Their roots slither through the mud and lift to form the tunnel walls. Neither fire nor iron shall be strong enough to escape them.

I can sense hunters in the distance. They have learnt not to stalk humans, the cost is too high for so meagre a meal. My spirit is in them as their howl reverberates through the trees and the ground trembles.

The human drops his tool, spinning to his feet. He clutches something at his belt, a metal claw which glimmers in the mist-light as he holds it out before him. I can see now the plant he was stealing from me - salus vita. I gave it to the humans once, showed them how to use the liquid from its tender stems to clean their wounds and how to chew its leaves to relieve their pain. They stole so much from me, the herb has almost vanished from my domain.

With it gone, my folk will suffer pain without relief, cursed by human greed.

Anger, hot as lighting, lances through me, ripping a snarl from my throat. How dare he plunder me? He turns again, presenting me with his back, his neck, his spine. Darkness clouds my vision and the air feels like steam in my lungs. It is a struggle to hold this form. I am the forest. I am the storm. Static crackles in the air, rippling my fur. My lips curl in a snarl like the roll of thunder. I coil and spring.

He drops under my weight. My claws tear at his flesh. I shift, warped by fury at this imposter - eagle's talons, bear's claws, wolf's teeth. I force myself back to the form of a lynx. My teeth snap at his shoulders and rip away the skin of my child that he wears. He twists under me and thrusts his claw upwards. I leap aside, the metal slicing tufts of hair from the tip of my ear. This one is fast!

As he stabs towards me, I catch his arm in my mouth, antici-pating the sanguine taste of victory. But the metallic tang across my tongue is not blood. A whimper bubbles in my throat. Iron. I clamp down hard, determined to wrest this armour from his body and shred his accursed flesh, no matter the pain it causes me. He writhes beneath me like a salmon crushed between a bear's jaws.

Sharp teeth burst from his arm. When did humans learn to shift as I can? They rend my mouth and I fall back with a snarl.

As we circle each other, I notice he favours his right side and the coverings of his left leg are dripping viscous crimson. My chest swells with triumph. Then I see my precious salus vita crushed under his heel. Fury grips me and all I see is red… He has taken life from my forest. Now he must die.

* * *

The Demon launches at me, and I barely escaped its tooth-filled jaw. My bracer, scarcely holding up against its raw strength. I press into my palm, fretting for the small leather loop. Where is it? More pressure…If I don't grab it in time, my arm will be lost. I try to look at the creature as I struggle. It is not a bear like the victim of the last attack reported. It is--Every time my mind tries to form a word to describe what I see, I cannot. The demon filters in and out of the ether. But it is real. The gash to my leg confirms it.

Got it! The loop I desperately searched for caught my finger. I swing my middle finger inside, barely latching it around my finger-tip, and flicked upwards. There is a frustrated growl as the creature detaches its hold and leaps back. The small metal blades on my forearm drip with a viscous translucent liquid, its hue slowly deepening into a familiar crimson. Blood?

If it bleeds, then it can be killed.

I struggle to stand. My leg…I need to patch it before infection sets in. I can use the salus vita I just found. Where did it go?

The creature and I circle each other. My leg burns with every step. Wait? Is that thing proud? The shifting image before me raises what seems like a head in a thrilled manner. I stepped back, losing my balance, hearing a crunch beneath my heel. The salus vita…crap!

The creature launches at me, a new rage enthralling it further. My knife is within reach. I dive for it as the creature soars above my head. Seconds is all I have. I roll to my back, as the demon hurtles towards me again, claw extended. I pull up my knife, nicking what I made out to be a foot. There is a small yelp, confirming I made contact. The creature licks its injured foot, and limps away back into the brush.

That was too close.

I roll to my knees and pull myself to the nearby boulder. My old muscles burn as I struggle to my feet. The leather around my leg is seeping blood. I need to clean the wound.

Gazing at the scuffed up ground, I finally find the goal of my endeavours. The herb. Now all I need is water. Gathering my bow and arrows, I let the sounds of the woods fill my ears. At first it's small, barely audible. A small trickle of liquid hitting rocks. Yes, over there.

Dragging my injured leg, I make my way to the blessed water that will save me from a slow death. I trudged along, keeping an ear out for the river, while remaining focused on the dark underbrush for the demon that still lurks within.

The light is dim amongst the pine and maple trees. Autumn is already in its early stages, the leaves just beginning to transfer into a series of gold and red. Had I not been in the middle of a hunt, and frankly, bleeding out; I would have enjoyed this scenery. In my youth, when my father first brought me to the woods, I was scared. He showed me that if we respect the woods, the forest spirit takes care of us in turn. Like magic, an old maple released almost all its leaves in the cool breeze. Red and gold fluttered down around me, as I danced in the falling foliage.

How long have I been walking? My mouth is beginning to feel parched, my tongue sandpaper behind my lips. I should have been there by now. It was almost as if the woods themselves were funnelling me away from the river I sought.

I continue on…I know the river is near. Gah! What was that?

I pull my leg forward, only to find it will not move. Something cold and rough creeps up my calf. I turn to look at what ensnares me. A branch? I bend down and pull the tangled vine from my leg. Just as it is removed, another grows up from the ground. What is this witchery? Frantically, I rip at the vines. Beating them down with my knife as they reach up for me.

Panic sets in. The forest is attacking me. Why? How deep does the monster's corruption go? I thrash and pull against the tangling branches. They grow faster than I can cut them. I need to keep moving, straining every muscle, it is my only chance.

Sickening snaps of the branches as they break begin to overshadow the sound of the water I desperately seek. Just ahead, there's an opening in the trees. Screaming, I will myself forward, finally reaching the edge, rolling, tumbling onto soft grass.

My heart races, and I frantically turn back toward the trees. The branches and vines are gone. The air is tight returning to my lungs. I scan my surroundings, gathering my yew bow and what arrows remain in my quiver. Light. Golden rays of sunshine warm my skin, brighter than the other areas of the woods. I closed my eyes, relishing the cosy welcome. It is the spirit of the forest, I am sure. The feeling of dread that was over me since I first stepped into the woods is gone.

There, through the clearing, is the river I sought. As I near the tranquil waters, there is a small tree bearing luscious red apples. My stomach growls upon seeing the round morsels. This is a gift from the great spirit, I am sure. I reach up and pull down two, rubbing their skin against my furs, bringing out their shine.

I struggle with the sack tied on my lower back. This was easier when I was younger. Finally pulling the string, the bag unfurls, dropping my small pot and cookware to the ground. I pull the salus vita from my inner shirt. The leaves are bent and damaged. If I boil it, I could still get the healing properties that I need to continue my hunt. I get to work on the riverbank, setting up my fire.

* * *

I lick the blood from my paw as muscle and sinew knit together. A gash is left across the pad, glimmering silver, an iron scar that will now be forever part of me. It taints my forest. The trees scream in my mind and my creatures wail and gnash their teeth. I am them and they are me.

It may already be too late. I can feel my link to them waver as though a branch has been lopped from me.

A new sensation stirs within me. There have been so many since the humans came, since they corrupted the simple lore of the forest. There was no fear, no anger, no hope, no hate, before they came. Live and die. That's all there was.

This one starts in the pit of my stomach, chewing my stomach lining like a rabid dog. It spreads through my limbs. The air around me thickens. Sticks in my throat. Mists swirl around my paws, moist and cool against my fevered body. Every time I look at the human's bloody trail, the sensation grips me again and I cannot move. It reminds me of fear but it is something more.

Terror.

I heard a human use the word once. He'd been speaking of me, leaning low over a campfire, tongues of flame creating a flickering demon-shadow across his face. 'The forest is terrorising us.' I hadn't understood. He played the victim, as though he hadn't breached *me*. As though his kind weren't bent on destroying *me*.

I'd seen what terror meant in the second before I ripped out his throat. But I hadn't understood it until now.

I was not afraid of killing the human, nor was I afraid of the fight. The terror that poisoned me meant far more than a psaltry human life. In tracking him down, I risked losing all that I was. He had already sliced a sliver from me, weakening my connection to *my* forest.

For years beyond counting, there had been life and death and life again. But now, where my presence was no longer connected with the woods, there was only death.

If he harms me again, what might happen to my beloved forest? If I let him go, what harm might he and his kind return to do? He will take the last root of salus vita and my forest will wither and die. It is my duty to protect, and I will uphold it, whatever it may cost me.

Golden feathers replace fur, front legs widening to wings. A change I had made a hundred times, yet never before had I felt pain. Metal flows within me, molten through my hollowed bones. I spread my wings, stiff, disjointed, feathers snapping. My beak cracks open as I wretch. I despise what he has done to me, to my forest, my creatures. With a scream of frustration, I take to the air.

The terror, the reluctance, do not vanish, but I quash them down, acid churning in my belly.

I circle above the trees, beady eyes watching for any movement.

My creatures hide in the trees and the dirt as my shadow passes over them. Then I see a gap in the canopy where they beckon me in. I land on a stout pine, then drop to the ground. It is unnatural for this shape, but the trees loom too close for me to fight from the air.

The human is sitting on the riverbank, feet dangling above the rushing water. A curved branch of yew bound with hair sits at his side. Lying next to it are twigs fletched with feathers. On the rock next to him, he is burning slivers of wood. A fresh, green scent fills the air as he boils *my* salus vita with *my* riverwater.

Without his stolen furs, he looks small. Coverings of green, blue, and black give him the hue of one of my birds. Like my squirrels, he has collected nuts. They tumble from a pouch at his waist as he bends to splash water over his leg. Then he leans back, air misting around his head as he sighs. He glances over his shoulder and I shrink into the shadow of a pine.

Muscles shift and extend. Bones crack as my jaw elongates. Carnivorous incisors burst from my gums and I snarl. The mists consume the sounds, hiding my presence as I transform. Only the iron scar remains unchanged, resisting my magic. The pain of it spears through my leg still, but it is nothing compared to the anguish the humans have caused my forest.

The human hasn't sensed me. His shoulders slump and he turns his face to a thin trickle of sunlight. I have not allowed it entry yet it pierces the gloom. I must kill him, restore control over my domain.

I sense his enjoyment as his teeth pierce apple-flesh and he sucks at the juices.

"Great forest spirit, if you can hear me, I thank you for my meal."

My bounty is not for him. I gave it once freely and was betrayed. Pine needles litter the ground and prickle my paws, the tree's way of reminding me to fulfil my oath.

Wolves howl in the distance and I raise my head to add my voice to theirs. Before I can, a movement at the water's edge distracts me. A rabbit kitten lies in the mud, a human snare around its leg. I curse my weakened state. How could I have missed one of my creatures in distress? Ofttimes it is the lore of the forest. For another to live, someone must die so the hunter may feast on their flesh. But I always know.

The kit thrashes against its bindings. Its rear leg is bloody, the fur matted, and its mouth is torn from trying to bite through the snare. The human notices it at the same time I do, the half-eaten apple thudding to the ground. He jumps down from the rock and approaches the rabbit kit.

A growl escapes me. It is mine. A baby. Not something he must eat to live or wear to ward off winter's chill. Death must give life.

He kneels by the kit, resting a hand on its back. Its teeth sink into his leather gloves and I am proud of it. Another emotion humans taught me but one of the few I do not find alien. He pays it no heed, pinning the kit in place with one hand as the other works on the snare. When it is loose, he cups the kit to his chest despite its struggles. I stalk forward, wary of hurting the rabbit should he see me. If I pounce on him, I may crush it or he may snap its neck to keep it from me.

He limps back to his stone, checking the heated mixture of herb and water. There is a ripping sound then he dunks a strip of blue into the concoction. The rabbit kicks at him, its feeble legs beating uselessly against his metal-clad arm.

A poor dinner though it may be, I fear he does mean to eat it. Petty. Cruel to show it the fire. I stop in my tracks. It is the lore of the forest, no matter the anger broiling within me. Live and die. I cannot interfere between prey and hunter.

The human withdraws the strip of blue and squeezes hot liquid over the kit's injured leg. The baby whimpers but its scrambling ceases as the herb numbs its pain and wards off fevered infection. After rummaging within his covers, he takes out a large leaf of salus vita. He wraps the kit's leg, then sets it on the ground next to the half-gnawed apple.

I should kill him now. He is distracted, his back to me, and my kit is out of danger.

My kit is out of danger.

This human respects the lore and respects my forest. He used the herb as I intended when I taught his ancestors so many seasons

ago. He showed appreciation for my bounty. He rescued my creature from another human's trap. My rabbit kit mewls at his feet.
Gratitude, or as close as a beast can understand it.

A pine needle snaps under my foot, a warning against my inde-
cisive heart. The human hears, grabbing his curved yew branch and
feather-fletched twigs tipped with gleaming iron. He raises the yew,
an iron shard pointed straight at my heart.

The air between us stills, mists bridging the narrow gap. One of
us will go to the otherworld this day. I draw back my lips, baring my
teeth. My claws dig into the dirt as I crouch, ready to pounce. Our
eyes meet. I spring.

Closing my eyes, I search for my centre. The essence of the woods. I
need to hear it. A technique taught to me by my father, and his
father before him. The pounding pulse of my heart that radiated in
my ears subsides, replaced by the small rustle of leaves as the wind
passes through the thick canopy above, the running of water from
the nearby stream, the fluttering of small wings in the distance, a
soft beat in the sod. Note all of them. Find the sound out of place…
There!

I open my eyes, barely escaping the demon's maw. Pain surges
through my leg. I let out my held breath, clenching my teeth. I let
the discomfort distract me. I didn't see it. A claw.

Searing pain stabs into my ribs. The ground beneath me, gone.
My movement only stopped by abrupt pain in every muscle of my
back as it slammed into the hard surface of the tree that caught me.
I reach for my knife, nestled still in the waist of my belt.

The demon approaches quickly. I have no time to recover…
trapped between the tree and the creature. Every muscle burns as I
reach for my knife, nestled still in the waist of my belt. My mind
wanders to my village as the creature leaps again. No, not like this.
They are depending on me.

As the monster descends upon me, resembling a cougar with the
girth of a bear, my knife twists with my wrist. The familiar resis-

tance hits my hand, as the blade bores its way through flesh. I apply more pressure, ignoring the pain of the claws against my skin.

The strength of the monster wanes. Finally the woods will heal. The salus vita will grow again, and my village will be saved.

Its body hangs limp in my arms. Warm, viscous liquid pours out onto my clothes. The weight of the demon begins to dissipate, as its body returns to the ether.

There will be no trophy to return to the village with. I gaze on in awe. Portions of the forest floor where blood made contact with the ground begin to bloom. A bushel of salus vita rises up. I pick one as light begins to bleed through the trees.

Something is wrong. The small plant's leaves are already losing their luminous soft olive texture. Changing into yellow. It is dying…but why?

Looking up around me, there was a heaviness to the air. I can no longer sense the energy of the woods.

No no no…

The last vestiges of the creature's body filter away on the breeze. As it touches my skin, my heart knows.

Great forest spirit…what have I done?

Defensive Posture

Audrey T. Carroll

When Jess had a garden of their own, they planted it very carefully. They chose marigolds and basil to keep pests away, lavender to help the bees. The pièce de résistance was a birdbath set beside a brass birdfeeder. Jess did not expect much. Mostly, when they had their coffee by the kitchen window in the morning, they just wanted to watch some sparrows and robins and finches as the sun rose up over the fields. Their white whale was an indigo bunting, which happened to be Jess' favorite shade of blue.

Crows left gifts. Jess remembered hearing that somewhere. But it was like a fairy tale they could never track to its original source. Once or twice a red-winged blackbird had come by, but they were easily startled and never stayed for long. There were no crows, at least not in their yard, though they'd hear them around sometimes. What there were, however, were strange black birds with shrill calls and strange pale eyes and iridescent heads—grackles.

The first gifts were so innocuous that it took Jess a while to even notice them. Twigs and bark bits left in the feeder. These made Jess smile, like the grackles though them incompetent enough to need help building their nest.

A neighbor came by the one morning, raising his voice because Jess was attracting cowbirds even though the birds' presence definitely predated the feeder. He kept calling them ma'am (*Ma'am, those are brood parasites! Ma'am, they'll destroy the ecosystem here!*) despite Jess correcting him with their name. Eventually, he threatened to get an outdoor cat and left.

The more the grackles dove into the cracked corn and sunflower seeds, the bigger the twigs got. Eventually dried flowers appeared, too. Jess collected most of these into the empty shell of a walnut by their bedside.

One morning, Jess noticed that a grackle drank from the bird-bath, two more feeding at the same time. It was unusual for them to cooperate, to not chase one another off. When Jess went to fill the feeder after their first cup of coffee, Jess discovered another gift, no bigger than a pinky finger. Jess plucked it from among the white millet and milo seeds. It was hard, stained red, and a fleshy red in the middle. They realized, too late, what it was: a bone.

Cold Weather

Calla Smith

Winter and just the temperature that leaves a crude frost on the lawns sparsely scattered around the city. The windows of Mateo's ground-floor apartment were coated in a cold white layer of ice when he woke, and he left the stove burner on after heating up the water for his tea. He wanted nothing more than to slip back into bed.

He left his house later than he should have, as he did almost every day. Those ten minutes of tardiness would set a series of familiar events in place. The bus would pull away just as he arrived at the bus stop, and the next one wouldn't come for another twenty minutes. The hour-long ride downtown would be almost painful, and when he finally arrived at his office, he would collapse into his chair, exhausted. And so would begin the reports and Excel spreadsheets and meetings until it was time to make his way back home again in the dark.

But that morning something was different. When Mateo arrived at the iron post that marked the bus stop, the bus was pulling up, almost empty. He paid his usual fare and sat at one of the seats by the window where he could gaze out over the early morning streets as they rambled by.

The only other people were a family that sat together in the back, quietly swaying with the jerking movements of traffic. A few other passengers found their own spots, but the trip was calm, and the streets remarkably free of traffic for that time in the morning.

Until the bus screeched to a sudden halt. Out of the window, he could see the other vehicles also seemed to be frozen in place. It must be another protest, he thought, but he was close enough to his office that he rang the bell, and the driver opened the swinging doors for him to step out onto the pavement.

Even though the sun was out, the air seemed colder than it had that morning. Colder than it ever was. There were no drums or honking horns or blasting music. The silence made the hair on the back of his neck stand up.

Then he saw it. The widest avenue in the city had a huge crack down the middle exposing the layers of concrete, bricks, and pipelines that ran deep beneath. And on the edge, the passengers of the buses and the drivers of the cars stood, paralyzed in disbelief.

A trail of smoke issued from the fissure that divided the historical city center from the rest of the urban sprawl. He took a few steps closer but stopped. He didn't want to see whatever it was that had immobilized the rest of the onlookers. He didn't want to see if anyone had been stranded on the other side.

More smoke billowed out, and the ground trembled under his feet. The other side split farther apart and dislodged from the solid ground he was standing on. The tremors grew stronger, and he almost fell to the ground. He turned around to put some distance between himself and the steep edge, but he couldn't leave yet. So much of his life had passed in the office on the other.

He thought, as he watched the chunk of land drift away, that if he had been trapped over there, he would never have been able to go home again.

The newly-formed island drifted off into the river until it was out of sight. Mateo turned around and started to trudge home. Now, he thought, he could spend the rest of the day warm under the covers.

The Marten

Maddisen Pease

It's nine in the morning, and we've been traveling since five.

The trucks drop us on a deserted road that runs along the Canadian border, in the middle of a forest a few miles from the mountain burning with 140,000 acres of wildfire we'd been sent to contain.

I am on my ninth season as a wildland firefighter on a crew of twenty other men, most of whom I'd worked with since I started this job fresh out of high school. The few rookies peppered among the group look fresh faced and sunken. I know what they're thinking, because I thought the same thing every day during my first season: what the hell am I doing out here?

"The fire is spreading east," Johnson says. He pulls out a pencil and a map from his shirt pocket. "This is where we are." He draws a circle. "They've got four other crews down there, including one all the way out from California. Even called in the National Guard, but we can't count on them until tonight." He makes X's where the other crews are stationed. I chew on a Slim Jim from my pack. "We're digging lines at the base of the mountain." More X's. He yammers on, heckling the rookies between briefing. When he finishes, he slips the map and pencil back into his pocket. "Alright, let's get to it."

We shoulder our packs and begin the long hike up the hill by the road, clearing brush and fallen branches as we go. The rookies wheeze, tottering beneath their packs as they lug chainsaws and axes up the hillside. Through the breaks in the tree canopy, I see the thick columns of smoke rising from the fire.

By noon we crest the hill, and I'm able to see the mountain and valley burning below. Flames raze a jagged line across the mountainside, and smoke plumes above, turning the cloudless blue sky an ashy gray. Two helicopters whir over the mountain, dropping sheets of water through the wall of smoke. We start down the hill, skittering over loose dirt, tripping over rocks and low branches. The wind picks up once we leave the tree line, drawing closer to the mountain's base. The smoke thickens. The rookies cough and spit, chugging water as we walk.

"They'll learn not breathe like the rest of us by the end of the season," Lynch says, coming up beside me. I've worked with Lynch for five seasons now, and I like him well enough. He smacks a horsefly on his neck. "God, I hate Montana. Didn't you grow up here, Kit?"

"Somewhere around here, yeah," I reply. This is the closest I've been to my former home in fifteen years. Time and fire have changed the landscape, but I know the mountain and my heart hurts to see it burning again. "When I was a kid, it was a camper's cigarette butt that lit the mountain on fire. That was the last time I was here. We moved right after."

We hike on. Lynch heckles the rookies, and my mind slides back to my thirteenth summer. It's the one I remember more clearly than all the others. It was the summer of the Marten, the summer of the fire, and the last summer I'd spent as a goblin child, free and dirty, with no regard for the future or the anxieties it might hold.

* * *

Before the sun comes up over the mountain, the early morning light filters through the curtains blue and hazy, reducing the room's contents to shadows. The first few minutes after waking are my favorite part of the day. I don't have to squint in order to see, and the world is quiet except for my heartbeat and the birds chattering outside my window.

It's my cue to get up when I hear the crunch of gravel in the driveway as my mother pulls in after her shift at the nursing home. I dress in the clothes crumpled on the floor by my bed, where I'd stripped them off the night before, then slip out my bedroom window to the forest behind my house.

I hike across the creek and up a hill, shivering in the morning chill that won't last through the hour. Two years previously, I'd built a fort a couple miles from the creek, and it's my favorite spot to watch birds and hunt for lizards, climb trees and read books I'd stolen from the library in the spring. The fort is built from two wooden boards nailed to a tree with a tarp thrown over, in a clearing surrounded by rosehip bushes and pine trees. It's not much, but I'm immensely proud of it. It protects the books from the rain and shields me from the sun on hot days.

Today, when I reach the fort mid-morning, it's torn apart. The tarp hangs lopsided from the wooden boards, and pages from books are scattered across the clearing among half-chewed granola bars and overturned plastic bins.

The culprit is a weaselly looking animal sniffing through the wreckage. Its fur is sleek and brown, except for a blond patch on its chest. Its face is pointed, ears perky. It moves nimbly, like a cat, but freezes when it sees me at the edge of the clearing.

Our gazes lock. For a moment my vision sharpens, and I know what it is to see clearly as its bottomless black eyes stare straight into mine. My breath catches, but then a bird chitters, and the spell is broken. The animal slinks away, into the safety of the trees.

I am not technically allowed at the library, but the next morning I go anyway.

The librarian, an ancient woman by my thirteen year old standards, has a short temper for children who repeatedly return stolen books with Cheeto stained pages and spines filled with dirt. I've racked up too many late fees to check out more books, and I don't pay them, so I resort to thievery, although I reckon that's something I would've done without the fees sooner or later to avoid being scolded by that old woman.

I slip silently through the stacks, keeping one eye trained on the desk where the librarian stamps incoming books. I pull half a dozen books on the North American weasel family and mammals of Montana and the Pacific Northwest. I spread them out on the floor, flipping through them until I find what I'm looking for: a slinky brown weasel with beady eyes and a blond chest. It is very cute, I have to admit. I slip the book under my shirt and dart out the door, giggling when I hear the old woman shouting after me.

When I return to my fort later that afternoon, it's waiting for me, perched on a tree branch above the roof.

"You're a pine marten," I tell it. The Marten blinks. "And according to this book, you're kind of endangered, which means I can't wallop you over the head for trashing my fort."

"I don't know what 'endangered' means," it responds. I jump. It spoke! "And I never heard of being a pine marten in my entire life."

"Y-you—you talk?"

"Sometimes."

"You speak English?"

The Marten leaps from the branch onto the roof. "You could have asked me my name, you know."

"Animals don't talk!"

"Well maybe they just don't talk to you," the Marten counters. "Or maybe you just don't listen."

"So what do you call yourself, if you don't go by pine marten?"

The Marten lets out a series of chitters that I can't replicate.

I shrug. "Still gonna call you Marten."

I suppose a part of me finds it strange that I'm speaking with an animal. Am I crazy? Is this a dream? Something a little like pride flares up within me. Just like in all my fantasy stories and comic books, something is *finally* happening to me. It might not be super strength or wizard powers, but I *am* speaking with an animal. I pinch my arm in case this is a dream, but I remain in the forest.

The first thing the Marten teaches me how to do is hunt. It skitters up a tree, crouching on a high branch quiet and still, watching a squirrel scamper up the tree beside it. I sit on the fort's roof, squinting through the blurriness that always accompanies my vision.

The squirrel crosses to the Marten's tree, pausing on the branch below the Marten. The Marten's tail swishes. I watch, transfixed, as the Marten bares its teeth, and with the swiftness of a cat it leaps, catching the squirrel in its claws and tearing into the neck with one fluid motion. Blood spurts, splattering the tree and staining the Marten's jaws red.

When the Marten finishes the squirrel, we climb trees and scamper over rocks deeper into the forest. It shows me hidden nooks and caves I'd never find on my own.

"Avoid this one in the winter," it tells me as we peer into one of the caves. "Bears."

I pick rosehips and we gorge ourselves on berries. The Marten hunts again and in the evening, before I return home, we swim in the creek.

The Marten is waiting on its perch above the fort when I return to the clearing every morning. We explore, and the Marten hunts, but by late afternoon my head starts to ache from squinting to see, and I have to lay down for a nap in the fort. After a week, the Marten becomes comfortable enough to curl into my side as I sleep.

June becomes July, which melts into August.

"I have to go to school soon," I tell the Marten one day. I start in two weeks, and I need the Marten to know I'm not intentionally abandoning it. "I won't be able to visit every day, but I can come on the weekends."

"What is school?" the Marten asks.

I dangle upside down from a tree, watching the Marten stare at a hole beneath a log. "It's where I go to learn things, like how to read and do math. Believe me, I'd much rather be here with you."

"You already know how to read," it replies. "And I don't know what math is, but it sounds boring."

"It is," I agree. "But I still have to go to school. If I don't, my mother says they will throw her in jail."

"Who is 'they'?"

"I dunno. The police, probably."

The Marten sniffs, then shoots under the log, rolling back out a moment later with a dead mouse in its claws. "You should run away." It tears into the mouse. "Live in the fort. I'll hunt squirrels and mice for you to eat."

I pull myself up, then climb off the tree. "I'm going, Marten. I'm going to school in two weeks." The Marten finishes the mouse, and we swim in the creek together like we always do, but when I return to the fort for my nap it does not follow.

The Marten is still gone by the time I wake. My mind feels thick and my thoughts come back slowly. For a moment I don't know where I am, because the air smells different and the inside of the fort, usually dim, is brightened with spots of bright light coming in through the crack between the tarp and the walls.

Is it morning already? Did I sleep through the night? Is my mother worried that I didn't return home?

Then I register the crackle and spit of flames on dry under-brush. I scramble up. The strange smell, I realize, is smoke from burning pine. I push the flap of the tarp away from the entrance, revealing the ring of fire that surrounds the clearing.

* * *

We dig the line with our faces three feet from the fire. Heat envelopes us. Smoke curls up in thick tendrils, stinging my eyes and snaking under the mask that covers the bottom half of my face, which is slick with sweat. My glasses slip down my nose. Beside me, a rookie wheezes.

When everything burns, nothing else in the world matters except the fire before me, the men digging beside me, and Johnson's faint hollers to the rookies behind me. The other crews are nothing but shadows to me as they pass by.

The blaze tinges the sky orange, smudged with shoots of spindly black trees. I stop twice for water. Six hours after we start digging, a four mile trench curves around one side of the fire. Helicopters continue dropping sheets of water. Other crews move forward, deeper into the blaze, some wetting the line my crew dug, others starting smaller, easily contained fires to burn up the fuel the wildfire chases.

"Take a break, eat something, drink some water," Johnson shouts. His blue eyes shine like beacons from a face streaked in black. Ash flecks his beard.

I turn away from the fire like the rest of my crew, steeling my aching body toward the long hike out when I hear the scream.

It shoots down my back, the familiarity of it making me shiver despite the heat. Time folds in on itself: Suddenly I am a thirteen year old boy again, but in the body of a man, flung back to the past, to a different fire on the same mountain. My crew hikes away without me. Against my better judgement, and the protests of my aching body, I leap over the trench into the fire.

I stumble blindly in the direction of the scream, a keening wail that cuts through the roar of the blaze and the crackle of burning trees. My eyes sting. Everything blurs, edged in shimmering heat and black smoke.

How far have I gone? I weave around flaming trees, crossing through memories back into reality, over and over again. Here: the copse of boulders where the firefighters found my exhausted body, still shouting for the Marten when I was thirteen. More stumbling, more screaming. There: the creek where we used to swim, where I last saw the Marten. I splash across it, and once again I am back in my childhood clearing, surrounded by a ring of flames sixty feet high.

I find the Marten huddling beneath a small boulder. Its black eyes glint in the darkness, reflecting the fire behind me. I get on my stomach and wriggle forward, reaching my hands into the hole. "It's been a while buddy," I say. "I hope you remember me."

The Marten blinks.

"I'm not leaving you again. I promise. Come on." The Marten sniffs my hand, whimpering. I grab the scruff of its neck and pull it out from under the boulder, cradling it against my chest.

When I cross back over the trench, time slots again, layering the present with more memories:

My crew, surrounding me with oxygen masks and bandages with the same practiced surety as the firefighters that rescued me as a child. Johnson, slapping me on the back, shouting, "Kit, you crazy son of a bitch." Then a flash memory of my mother, sobbing, as she pulls me into her arms. "Kit, don't you ever worry me like that again!" Someone puts a blanket over my shoulders, and for a moment I don't know which fire I just came out of. The faces of my crew are blurred. I can't see. Where are my glasses? "Kit!" Lynch shouts, as if from a distance. "Kit!" My mother, crying again as she searches me for scratches and burns.

"My face hurts," I try to say, but I don't know if anyone hears me. Someone takes the Marten out of my arms. Johnson leads me away from it, towards a medic.

The Marten chitters, begging me to come back, but I'm already gone.

* * *

They take the Marten to a wildlife clinic about thirty miles from Missoula. I don't know who. I drive there on my day off, a week after I pulled the Marten out of the fire. I don't even know if wild animals are allowed to have visitors, but I have to know that it's okay. The sky is still hazy, but I can see the blue . On the horizon, dark storm clouds gather, promising rain.

"I'm here to see the pine marten that was brought in about a week ago," I tell the woman behind the front desk. I shift nervously as she looks me up and down, her gaze lingering on my singed eyebrows, and the healing burn that stretches from my hairline to the tip of my nose. My glasses are bent, a secondary pair dug from the bottom of my pack.

"You must be the firefighter that pulled him from the fire," she says. I nod. "Follow me."

She leads me down a hall and into an exam room. She tells me to wait, coming back a few minutes later with the Marten wrapped in a blanket and cradled like a cat in her arms. The Marten's legs are bandaged, its fur singed. She lays it gently on the table in the center of the room.

"In addition to his burns and a broken leg, he breathed in a lot of smoke. His lungs are practically shot to hell, and the vet wants to put him down, but your boss called and asked us to keep him comfortable until you got here." She lays a hands on my shoulder and offers a small smile. "He's old for a pine marten. About twenty years old, as far as we can figure."

"Thank you," I say. I pull a chair over to the table. I set my hand, loosely curled into a fist, in front of the Marten's nose. It sniffs me, then closes its eyes. I rest my chin beside its head, breathing in its clean scent of dish soap and the faintest of pine. Its tail flicks, and I know it's saying hello, even if we can't speak with the woman watching us.

I'm sorry, I tell the Marten silently. *I'm sorry I left you all those years ago.* I stroke its head with the pad of my thumb.

Its tail flicks again. Forgiven.

I don't know how long we sit together like that, but eventually I look up and realize that the woman from the front desk has returned with another person dressed in blue scrubs. The vet, I'm guessing.

The vet smiles at me. "When you're ready," they say, and my gaze flicks to the syringe filled with clear liquid that they hold gingerly.

The Marten opens its eyes and looks straight into mine. It blinks. We both know it's time. I press my forehead to the Marten's. Its fur is soft against my burn. "Goodbye friend," I whisper. Its nose nudges my cheek.

The vet steps forward and presses the needle into the Marten's neck. "This will help him sleep. No more pain."

I breathe in. I breathe out. The Marten's black eyes turn glassy, and then its body stills. I press one last kiss on its head and get up to leave, acutely aware of how hard my heart is beating, and how wet the tears are that slide down my cheeks.

Creative Non-Fiction

When sunlight meets a tree

Milena Filipps

Every evening, a ray of sunlight descends to a forgotten garden and leans on a tree. This tree is young and thin compared to its peers standing a bit further away, still wearing their heavy coats of dark leaves at the end of summer. All those leaves, much larger than my hands, sing an old hymn that is instantly picked up by wind and carried away to places much different from a green idyll.

When sunlight meets a tree, it falls on a trunk that has not witnessed a whole century yet, but it has heard the wind speak almost every day for the last few decades. A ray of sunlight never brings a song to sing, a ballad to recite, a melody to whisper – and so the leaves of every tree, pale and dark, green, brown and yellow, remain indifferent to its presence, as much as they do not care about their own shadow. They barely notice this grey phantom stretched on the ground beneath them, sometimes imitating the shape of two specific branches, just like a ghost may imitate the voice once attributed to the name on the ghost's gravestone. Sunlight experiments with this shape, as the wind forms the language of trees. The grey spot on the ground may be as transparent as a fallen cloud, or marked by edges as sharp as if they were drawn by an architect's pencil. A quiet companion as familiar as the restless air.

Our own thoughts envy the variety and beauty of the evening's colour and the fleeting contrasts sunlight paints in the garden. We interpret them as a synthesis of change and eternity, two strange concepts we admire for providing a clear dichotomy, ready to be projected on all particularities of life, such as a broken watch, a dying flower or an abandoned garden. Becoming accessible and yet mysterious when reflected by art.

Sunlight only ever leaves the tree to rest at night. It is there to make its drawings in the earliest morning hours, but for some reason we choose to believe the evening to be the time of a long-awaited meeting, most probably because of a random impression we once stumbled upon at that hour and then put on a pedestal. Yet beauty is not the only paradigm capable of guiding our perceptions. There may be another reason why we are so drawn to that visible collision of time and time, growth and passing, roots once laid in the earth by a gardener and a ghostly substance without any clear shape. As we watch the sunlight lay on a tree's shoulder, we cannot see beyond our sad, boring, conventional, static dreams, yet we sense the imperfections of our own mind and the art it produces. Thus, we cling to a question, the need for a final decision. What is this place to our thoughts - a garden or a graveyard?

A Fine Bright Line

Patty Somlo

We had made our way down unpaved gravel roads before, so this one, fifty miles outside Kanab, Utah, didn't appear especially daunting. The nice older man at the local visitor center, wearing a large white cowboy hat, plaid Western shirt with white piping, and jeans, had already assured us this road was passable with non-four-wheel-drive cars.

When my husband Richard turned off the highway and the road switched from dark gray pavement to pale gray gravel atop reddish-tan sand and dull brown dirt, I saw the sign. The speed limit was now twenty-five.

A few minutes later, Richard slowed down to twenty. We hit a wash-boarded section and it became impossible to talk, our voices turning jittery and garbled. Richard couldn't go faster than fifteen now.

Our Honda SUV had entered the Vermillion Cliffs National Monument. Unlike the nearby national parks, Zion and Bryce, this protected federal land contained few developed roads or services. I hoped we would encounter less people than in the overrun sections of the national parks. This also meant if something bad happened, we would be stuck.

I know there is a fine bright line when it comes to wilderness. On one side is the opportunity to take in unrivaled splendor -- of stately ancient trees, rushing streams and waterfalls, and snow-covered peaks -- matched by remarkable silence, broken only by sweet bird sounds and occasional rustling leaves. But to have this experience without other people usually entails going to a place not easily accessible. That adds an element of danger.

Richard carefully maneuvered the car around treacherous-looking rocks and down smooth stretches, then gunned the engine to rush up before the tires got swallowed by sand. I noticed there was no longer cell service. I calculated the distance we had gone and how long it might take to walk back.

Momentarily, I considered suggesting we turn around. There was a decent chance we could make it back. But since we'd gone this far, why not continue and see what we'd come for?

We had come to see for free what otherwise would have cost us. Not far from the trailhead where we were headed was another path leading to The Wave, rolling red-pink rock made popular two decades ago by a German traveler. The photographs he took were widely shared. These days, the Bureau of Land Management that oversees the monument restricts access, requiring visitors to get one of the twenty permits issued each day, ten of which go to outdoor guide companies that charge steep fees.

Usually, government agencies managing wilderness areas provide warnings, of bears, infected rodents and ticks, or advice to stay on the trail. In these stunning varicolored rock landscapes of Southern Utah, the warnings are about getting stuck, trapped in a flash flood that can start without warning from a sudden downpour or lost on these unpaved roads, lacking water, in the scorching summer heat. Every year, people die out here. I thought about this each time we hit an especially bumpy section and Richard, who likes to drive over the speed limit, slowed the car to ten miles an hour.

To calm us down, I threw this out. "We're going to get there, and the parking lot's gonna be full."

Richard laughed.

"You're probably right."

I couldn't count the times during the twelve years Richard and I lived in Oregon that we ventured out some poorly maintained gravel road to hike on a trail leading to a lake or a wildflower-strewn mountain meadow. The further we went beyond the safety of the paved highway, the more I assumed we were alone. Yet, the trail-head parking lot would always be filled with cars.

Fortunately, we made it to the parking lot on this day without getting stuck in sand or bursting a tire on a sharp, protruding rock. The large lot was half-full.

After pulling into the last vacant space on the west side, Richard and I stepped out of the car. Before we had a chance to retrieve our hiking boots from the back, a guy in a floppy canvas hat walked up. He was talking while he walked, as if an invisible companion accompanied him. I grabbed my boots, walked up front, and sat down. As I looked out the window, I couldn't tell if the guy was talking to Richard or himself.

Since he spoke fast, I only picked up occasional words, something about the nerve of the government to charge fees, when there wasn't a developed trail here. If Richard didn't cut him off, he might go on all day.

I tied the laces on my olive-green hiking boots, got out of the car and walked over to where Richard was standing. The guy was still talking, as if his words were on a loop, replaying over and over again. Eventually, I gleaned a couple of points. As there was no official trail, we would be hiking down the middle of a dry creek bed wash. To reach the colorful rock formation we'd been promised at the visitor center, we would need to climb up or down a wall. To avoid this barrier, our talkative friend said we should detour up a side trail, found near some structures called "the domes." In addition to being easier, skirting around the domes would afford a spectacular view, which we couldn't get if we followed the dry creek bed, as the other suckers who'd left their cars in the parking lot were apt to do.

Richard and I started out on the wide dusty wash, bordered by walls of desert-shaded rock. After the treacherous drive, it was a letdown. We had been staying in this part of Southern Utah for two weeks and seen stunning sights. I'd probably become jaded by now.

The scenery didn't change or improve as we walked. Richard and I searched for the side trail, repeating the sparse directions the guy had shared. Every so often, other hikers passed, headed for the parking lot. Eventually, it seemed we'd gone too far.

"It must be back there," Richard said, pointing in the direction from which we'd come.

"Do you want to go back?" I asked.

"I guess so."

On the way in, I had noticed several large, rounded lumps of dark brown stone high above the wash. I realized these might be "the domes." Hard as I'd searched, though, I couldn't recall having seen a trail leading up to them.

We retraced our steps, glancing left, in the direction of the domes, as we walked. Every so often, what looked to be a narrow path veered uphill. We tried following several of these slender byways, with Richard making me go first as the scout. Each narrow dusty path dead-ended not long after it started.

Finally, one path did keep going, and I followed it. Even though I was hungry and hot, I felt determined to reach the glorious view-point, where we could sit down and eat our lunch.

At one point, the trail suddenly narrowed, with high rock walls closing in on both sides. The temperature cooled. This was the only place we'd encountered shade the entire morning. Even though we hadn't found the view, this looked like a good spot to sit out of the sun and eat sandwiches we'd brought.

"Are you hungry?" I asked Richard.

"I am. You want to eat here?"

"Yes."

I looked around until I found a rock bench that appeared long and wide enough for us to sit. But it suddenly occurred to me to step away from the narrow passageway and get a better look.

"Just a minute," I said to Richard. "I want to look at something."

I followed the trail out to where the high walls became lower, and finally ended, and the path opened up. I turned around.

"Oh, my God," I said.

I hurried back to where Richard sat on the rock.

"This is it," I said.

"What?"

"This looks like what we saw in the photo at the visitor center."

Richard got up and followed me out of the cool dark shade, along the trail into the sun. He turned around and looked back to where he'd been sitting.

"You're right," he said. "Wow."

The rock surrounding our lunch spot was pink, and smooth as a piece of shaped and fired pottery. The hard surface, whose hue ranged from pale rose to dark mauve, bordering on lavender, appeared charred by fire in some places or having had black paint spilled down. The pink stone flowed like liquid, in layers, above and alongside the path.

Richard hurried back and set his sandwich down on the rock, then returned to where I stood and started snapping photographs.

After lunch, we climbed three more faint trails. Each one dead-ended, without leading to the view our parking lot guide had promised. Finally, a fourth trail kept going up, so I followed it, certain that just above the next hill we would reach the edge and marvel at the stunning vista. Each time I crested another hill, though, the ground leveled out, stretching farther than I could see, in whatever direction I looked. Richard suggested we give up. I reluctantly agreed.

As I picked my way down, I soon got lost. We were no longer on the path we'd originally followed up. To find the way, I retraced my steps, and eventually landed on a wide rocky trail. I shaded my eyes and focused as far down as I could. Continuing down seemed like a good bet to get us back to the main wash.

On the way, I wondered if the guy in the parking lot was for real or not. Perhaps, he was a trickster, the sort of character you might find in an oft-repeated Native American tale. Then I had to ask myself, if his story about the side trail to a glorious view was made up, what would have been the point?

That led me to consider the point of coming here at all. Why did anyone bother to go to far-flung places, when nearly everything was available to us virtually, on TV or the Internet?

Once when Richard and I had just arrived at the Paradise visitor center in Mount Rainier National Park, I watched two middle-aged couples take turns snapping photographs of one another. They stood in front of the visitor center, making sure to get Mt. Rainier's snow and glacier-covered top into the background. After each couple had posed for several photographs, I overheard one of the men say, "Okay. We've got proof that we've been here."

I know a couple that travels often. Whenever we're at a dinner party with them, they rehash their latest trips. Instead of describing what they saw or enjoyed, they take turns, hopping from sight to sight and activity to activity, comparing their experiences with others at the table who've visited the same places, as in, "Did you stop at the waterfall?" or "We did the zip-line over the canyon. Did you?" As I listen, I wait to hear some amazement or wonder at what they've seen, or gratefulness that such beauty exists. I rarely hear this.

The biggest attraction travel holds for me is the element of surprise. I often find that the unplanned aspects of a trip can lead to the most memorable moments. It excites me to stumble upon unexpected beauty that can't be packaged and sold.

Maybe the trickster wanted to mess with us, to make it impossible to reach the site, and keep us from bragging, comparing, or one-upping other travelers.

The wide path we took on our return cut both down and across, shortening the distance we'd covered going in. Before we knew it, we landed back at the parking lot.

On the way to the paved highway, I looked around. Unlike the trail, which had been a bit of a letdown, what I glimpsed of the Vermillion Cliffs National Monument on both sides of the road caused me to repeatedly gasp, "Wow."

The view stretched a long distance, even though we weren't at a high point, but level with the landscape. Smaller sandstone formations dotted the foreground, while tall, variegated cliffs framed the back. A palette of dark brown to tan, red to orange, and forest green to turquoise colored the rock and sand. This was an artist's dreamscape.

And then, when it seemed we must be close to the paved road, I spotted the greatest surprise.

"Oh, my gosh. Look at that," I shouted to Richard.

They appeared to be huge conical piles of finely crushed rock, created by a monster child playing in his football field-sized sandbox. The shades were pastel, running from darker to lighter and back again, and from wide bottoms to narrow, pointed tops. Nature had created a work of art.

Richard pulled off the gravel road, to where the shoulder widened. We got out of the car and walked to the first colorful pastel mound. A landscape photographer, my husband couldn't have been happier. Since he was studying the mounds to compose artful shots, I had a chance to wander.

As I took in the wondrous landscape of both pastel domes and the high, variegated mountains further back, I felt flooded by gratitude that places like this still existed, and it was possible to be here without tour buses and a hundred people taking selfies. Richard and I could experience this without a single other person in sight.

Then I thought about the trickster in the parking lot. I wondered if he intentionally forced us to wander, to open our minds to possibility and a willingness to search.

I tried to recall Native American stories I'd heard about Kokopelli, the hunchbacked flute player whose image adorns a pair of sterling silver and turquoise earrings I bought from a Navajo woman artist on the side of the road. A mythical Hopi symbol, Kokopelli is considered a fertility god, prankster, healer and storyteller. One legend has it that following winter, Kokopelli's music is what ushers in spring.

For a moment, I let myself imagine that I could hear his flute, playing a slightly mournful song. Once he had finished, I would look forward to hearing the stories he had to tell, about the magical place Richard and I were lucky enough to find.

The Swamp

Marisa Jade

We have all heard of stories of little boys and little girls coming up missing. Most of the time, we stare at our phones, ignore the amber alerts passing by, and we assume that all those little boys and little girls are kidnapped, whisked away, held captive by an evil witch. But no one knows where those little boys and girls are or if they're even alive.

I know the tale of a young girl that discovered a swamp for the first time.

This little girl arrived at her old childhood home in Cape Coral, Florida. The house was rugged and painted yellow. The little girl dressed like a Disney princess. She wore a Cinderella dress with matching plastic heels and a tiara.

She entered the house.

The house seemed oddly familiar. The house looked like the little girl's house, but the house was completely pitch black. The only light that shined was the little girl herself.

The little girl started walking down the hallway where her dad's home studio used to be, where her little brother's bedroom used to be (did she have a little brother? She could not remember), where the family bathroom used to be, and, finally, her bedroom.

She slowly opened her bedroom door. There, she discovered a swamp for the first time in her life.

The little girl was petrified. Her room was completely flooded by darkness, water, spiders, snakes, alligators, and crocodiles. The little girl could even see cobwebs and shadows with big white eyes and pearly demonic teeth.

Her room contained all the things she feared the most.

Suddenly, the water started to pour out of her room. The little girl ran as fast as her little legs could go. The little girl ran, crying and screaming with all her might, until...

Unfortunately, I do not remember the rest of the tale.

Did the little girl die?

Did she drown?

THAT, I do not remember.

Author Biographies

Farrah Lucia Jamaluddin (she/her) is an unpublished writer, poet and late bloomer, born in England and currently living in Italy with her partner and Maltese terrier. She is currently studying a BA in psychology and philosophy, in between her determination to learn Italian and make pizza. She enjoys magical realism, and post-colonial studies, as well as painting in watercolour. She can be found on Instagram and Medium writing about love, intersectional feminism, and challenging the status quo.

Kelsey Lister is an emerging poet residing in Alberta, Canada. With work appearing in *Maudlin House, Anti-Heroin Chic, Paddler Press, Roi Fainéant Press, Moss Puppy* & others, she is also an assistant poetry editor for *Parentheses Journal.* You can find her on Twitter @stolencoat

LeeAnn Olivier, MFA, is the author of *Doom Loop Wonderland* (The Hunger Press, 2021) and *Spindle, My Spindle* (Hermeneutic Chaos Press, 2016). Her poetry has recently appeared in *The Missouri Review, Superpresent Magazine, Williwaw Journal,* and elsewhere. Originally from Louisiana, LeeAnn now teaches English at a college in Fort Worth, Texas. She is a survivor of domestic violence, breast cancer, and an emergency liver transplant.

Joseph M. Jablonski, also known as the Walking Mall Poet, is the typewriting street poet of Old Town Winchester, Virginia. Using one of the many typewriters in his collection, Joseph produces on-the-spot poetry by request for passerbys. Previously published works include Dropout, available from *Jafansta Press*, and individual works featured in *Five2One*'s #thesideshow and in *The Odyssey*. He has also been featured on The Auxoro podcast and in The Winchester Star.

Elijah Woodruff (He/Him) is a high school English teacher who doesn't do it for the money but wouldn't mind being paid a little more. He spends his free time drinking too much coffee and watching movies with his fiancée. His works have appeared/will appear in *Roi Fainéant* press, *Vocivia Magazine*, *Curio Cabinet Magazine* and *Coalition for Digital Narratives*. You can find him on twitter: @Woodrelli

Anushri is a poet and creative writing mentor. She writes to fight against her own mental health issues and to fight for everyone's collective mental health representation. She has spent half her life in one half of the globe and the other in the other half. She likes to think of herself as a permanent alien, alternatively a global citizen.

Ber Davis is a writer & poet from Wisconsin. Her written work has appeared in *Creatures Magazine, orangepeel literary magazine, Loud Coffee Press*, and elsewhere. She is currently channeling her creative energy into a coordinated, passionate study of art history & archival preservation.

Devon Neal (he/him) is a Bardstown, KY resident who received a B.A. in Creative Writing from Eastern Kentucky University and an MBA from The University of the Cumberlands. He currently works as a Human Resources Manager in Louisville, KY. His work has been featured in *Moss Puppy Magazine, Dead Peasant, Paddler Press, MIDLVLMAG*, and others.

. . .

Devon Webb is a 25-year-old writer based in Aotearoa New Zealand. She writes full-time, exploring themes of femininity, youth & vulnerability. She shares her poetry online, through live performance, & has been widely published both locally & internationally. She is the two-time Wellington Slam Poetry Champion & is currently working on the final edits of her debut novel, *The Acid Mile*. Her work can be found on Instagram, Twitter & TikTok at @devonwebbnz.

Jente H. is a non-binary writer and social worker from Belgium. They developed an interest for poetry and prose at an early age and does photography work on the side. In their free time, Jente is also the host of their selfmade podcast titled 'coffee & film' in which they discuss anything cinema related. Ko-Fi: ko-fi.com/horrorwild.

N.A. Kimber (she/her) is a writer from Caledon, Ontario. She has been writing since she was twelve years old and has always been moved by the power of storytelling across all mediums and genres. She is the co-founder of the online publication Forget Me Not Press which she runs with her twin sister and artist, K.E. Donoghue-Stanford. She can usually be found with a cup of tea in hand and either knitting, reading, or (obviously) writing.

Jasmine Young is a poet and creative writer residing in the northeastern corner of Vermont. If she could, she would spend every moment napping with her black cat, Oliver. You can find her on Instagram @nyctxnthus

Maria Grace Nobile is from New York City. Her work has been published in *Agape Review, Livina Press,* and *Poetry as Promised Literary Magazine. Jaden Magazine, Juste Literary,and The Expressionist Literary Magazine,* and it also appears in the anthologies, *Inked with Passion,* *and Love Letters to a Thousand Yesterdays, and Fate.* She loves writing poetry, both spiritual and prose, and in various languages. Twitter: MariaG.Nobilepoetry @gnovb2 and Instagram @marianobilepoetry

SOUM is an acronym for Screams Of Unfettered Minds, a collective of three women who write under the cloud of preferred anonymity. Their writing leans to the raw, unpolished, cheeky, punchy style, championing awareness to mental and social issues.

Diane Webster's work has appeared in "El Portal," "North Dakota Quarterly," "New English Review" and other literary magazines. She had a micro-chap published by Origami Poetry Press in 2022, and one of her poems was nominated for Best of the Net.

Jared Wong (he / him) lives in Whitehorse, Yukon and within the traditional territories of the Kwanlin Dün First Nation and Ta'an Kwäch'än Council. He has a BA from Mount Allison University, an MA from Carleton University and is an avid slurpee drinker and snow watcher. His work has appeared with *Horse Egg Literary, Impostor, 7Mondays, Bywords, Empyrean* and *Filling Station*, as well as on the underside of a million discarded post-it-notes.

Wren Donovan's poetry appears or is upcoming in *Poetry South, Orca, Chaotic Merge, Yellow Arrow, Harpy Hybrid Review*, and elsewhere in print and online. She studied at Millsaps College, UNC-Chapel Hill, and University of Southern Mississippi. When not writing, Wren reads Tarot and history books, practices dance meditation, and talks to cats. She lives in Tennessee. Links to published work: WrenDonovan.weebly.com.

. . .

Tim Murphy (he/him) is a disabled civil rights attorney, environmentalist, and poet who lives in Portland, Oregon. His writing explores the natural world, disability, and the climate crisis. Tim's work is featured in *Remington Review*, *Writers Resist*, and *The Long Covid Reader*, a book coming out this fall. Tim can be found on Instagram and Twitter (@brokenwingpoet).

Brandon Shane is a Japanese-American alum of California State University, Long Beach, where he majored in English. He's pursuing an MFA while working as a writing instructor and substitute teacher. You can see his work in the *Berlin Literary Review, Acropolis Journal, Grim & Gilded, Livina Press, Mister Magazine, Remington Review, Salmon Creek, BarBar Literary Magazine, Discretionary Love*, among others.

Joseph Blythe is a Yorkshire writer of prose, poetry and, occasionally, scripts. His poem 'Judas' was included in the Grist anthology *We're All In It Together: Poems for a DisUnited Kingdom* (2022) and his short story 'Meteor' will be included in their forthcoming collection *Apocalypse Now? Stories for the End of the World*. He is currently working on a poetry collection, an apocalyptic eco-novel novel and a literary novel surrounding memory. He tweets @wooperark and Instagrams @wooperark.

Holland Zwank is pursuing a degree in Creative Writing and Publishing at Northwest Missouri State University, is the office manager at GreenTower Press and has work in *Papeachu Press*.

When she isn't working in a research lab with her biology MS, **H.E. Shippas** can be found writing creative pieces, playing indie video games she helped fund, or trying new foods in Philadelphia, PA. She has previously been published in DSTL Art's Aurtistic Zine and The Shallot's Mental Health Magazine.

Ben Coppin (he/him) lives in Ely in the UK with his wife and two teenage children. He works for one of the big tech companies. He's had a textbook on artificial intelligence published, as well as a number of short stories, mostly science fiction, but also horror, fairy tales and other things. All his published stories can be found listed here: http://coppin.family/ben.

Jeff Presto is an author from Pittsburgh, Pennsylvania. He is a fan of all things horror and enjoys mountain biking in his spare time. His favorite authors include Chuck Palahniuk, Bret Easton Ellis, and Ray Bradbury. You can find him on twitter @signedinpen and on Instagram @signedinpen

Angela Patera is an emerging writer and published artist. Her short stories have appeared in Myth & Lore Zine, Iceblink Literary Magazine and a few more. Her art has appeared in numerous publications, as well as on the cover of Selenite Press and Penumbra Online. When Angela isn't creating, she likes to spend time outside in nature. You can find her on both Twitter @angela_art13 and Instagram @angela_art13

Ashley Mina strives to exist. She holds an Associate of Arts in Creative Writing and currently resides as a settler on the unceded land of the xʷməθkʷəy̓əm, Sḵwx̱wú7mesh, and səlilwətaɬ peoples (Vancouver, BC). Her work can be found locally printed in the NVDPL and published in The Liar Zine.

Jessica Ungeheuer (she/her) is a writer and artist. While earning her visual arts degree she studied creative writing and screenwriting. Her favorite genres are sci fi and horror. She lives in Bradenton

Florida with her fiance and two mischievous cats. You can find her on Twitter @phoenixfire110 and Instagram @phoenixfire110.

Alethea Lyons (she/ze) writes short- and long-form SFF, especially dark fantasy, folklore, science-fantasy, and dystopias. Her debut novel, The Hiding, comes out 5th March 2024. She lives with her husband, little Sprite, a cacophony of stringed instruments, and more tea than she can drink in a lifetime. https://linktr.ee/alethearlyons

Audrey T. Carroll is the author of What Blooms in the Dark (ELJ Editions, 2024), Parts of Speech: A Disabled Dictionary (Alien Buddha Press, 2023), and In My Next Queer Life, I Want to Be (kith books, 2023). She can be found at http://AudreyTCarroll Writes.weebly.com and on Twitter @AudreyTCarroll and Instagram @AudreyTCarroll

Calla Smith (she/her) grew up in Colorado, where she quickly discovered her love of reading, writing, and language. After completing a foreign exchange program in Argentina in high school, she went on several trips throughout South America before settling in Buenos Aires in 2009. There she worked as an ESL teacher while studying translation. She now enjoys city life in her adopted country and continues to explore her passion of writing.

Maddisen Pease is a writer and student at The Evergreen State College. When she's not writing, she enjoys reading romance novels, collecting records, and spending time with her cat June.

Milena Filipps is a history student in Germany. She enjoys reading works by Marcel Proust, Jane Austen and Goethe as well as learning about art history and historical architecture. Her essays "Academic Reading" (2023) and "My Glasses" (2023) were published by Livina Press, while her poems appeared in Swim Press (2023), The Field Guide Poetry Magazine (2023), RIC Journal (2021) and Mosaik (2020), among others. You can find her on Twitter @milenafilipps and Instagram @milenafilipps

Patty Somlo's most recent book, *Hairway to Heaven Stories*, was published by Cherry Castle Publishing, a Black-owned press committed to literary activism. *Hairway* was a Finalist in the American Fiction Awards and Best Book Awards. Two of Somlo's previous books, *The First to Disappear* (Spuyten Duyvil) and *Even When Trapped Behind Clouds: A Memoir of Quiet Grace* (WiDo Publishing), were Finalists in several book contests.

Marisa Jade is a recent graduate from Florida SouthWestern State College. She absolutely loves to write and aspires to become an independent self-published author. One thing she loves to do, besides reading and writing, is helping other authors reach success. She is currently working on her first novel. Her works have appeared in the Heart of Flesh, where she wrote a testimony, and the Chamber Magazine, where she wrote her first book review.

Printed in Great Britain
by Amazon